KU-485-665

The World of the Short Story

An Anthology Chosen by

ANDREW BEST AND MARK COHEN

With an Introduction by

ALLAN GRANT

LONGMAN

LONGMAN GROUP LIMITED
London

Associated companies, branches and representatives
throughout the world

Introduction and notes © Longman Group Ltd 1975

This edition first published 1975

ISBN 0 582 35116 2

Printed in Great Britain by
Western Printing Services Ltd
Bristol

The Heritage of Literature Series

The World of the Short Story

The Heritage of Literature Series

Founder General Editor: E. W. Parker, M.C.

The titles in this series include modern classics, and a wide range of prose, poetry, and drama.

Other titles in the Modern Classics section of the series include:

SUNSET SONG *Lewis Grassic Gibbon*
SCOOP *Evelyn Waugh*
THE GOSHAWK *T. H. White*
ANIMAL FARM *George Orwell*
THE WESKER TRILOGY *Arnold Wesker*
ROOTS *Arnold Wesker*
THE ROYAL HUNT OF THE SUN *Arnold Wesker*
THE LONELINESS OF THE LONG-DISTANCE RUNNER *Allan Sillitoe*
with BILLY LIAR *Keith Waterhouse*
GO TELL IT ON THE MOUNTAIN *James Baldwin*
EXCEPT THE LORD *Joyce Cary*
CRY, THE BELOVED COUNTRY *Alan Paton*
THE WAY OF ALL FLESH *Samuel Butler*
DARKNESS AT NOON *Arthur Koestler*
SATURDAY NIGHT AND SUNDAY MORNING *Alan Sillitoe*
THIS SPORTING LIFE *David Storey*
BRIDESHEAD REVISITED *Evelyn Waugh*

Other titles in the Short Stories section of the series include:

SCIENCE FICTION Edited by *S. H. Burton*
MODERN SHORT STORIES Edited by *S. H. Burton*
THIRTEEN SHORT STORIES Edited by *H. Bell*
SHORT STORIES OF THE TWENTIETH CENTURY Edited by *R. W. Jepson*
SHORT STORIES BY MODERN WRITERS Edited by *R. W. Jepson*

CONTENTS

INTRODUCTION

In making their selection of modern short stories, Andrew Best and Mark Cohen have cast their net very widely. They have included at least one representative story from as many different parts of the English-speaking world as possible. But geography was clearly not their only concern: at the same time I think they were insisting that good short stories are still being written everywhere, despite the sense that anyone who reads short stories for pleasure has that they are no longer fashionable reading.

There may be a number of different explanations for this situation, and one might begin with the disappearance, especially in England, of many of those literary periodicals in which short stories regularly appeared at a time when television was growing, not only as a medium of communication but, more importantly, as an expression of imaginative pleasure. More than a few writers who begin by writing fiction are easily persuaded into radio or television drama, where the immediate rewards are higher and the potential audience very large indeed. But television does not seem to have eroded the habit of reading. The evidence points the other way, and there may be a quite different kind of reason for the decline of the short story, which has more to do with literature and its audience than with the world of the mass media. Literature that readers recognize as modern is often marked by an appearance of novelty; literary experiment has provided much of the excitement of serious reading in the modern age since the early decades of this century at least. Regarded in this light the short story may appear unadventurous; its shape, if shape is the

vii

right word, achieved its definition in the nineteenth century somewhere between the *Tales* of the American writer, Edgar Allan Poe and the *Sketches* of Ivan Turgenev, the Russian novelist. Within the two general categories of the tale, with its brevity and conclusive point, and the sketch, often accidental and inconclusive in appearance, the short story has remained in the hands of many different kinds of writers like a set of endlessly occurring variations. Perhaps it is because the form so quickly achieved elasticity and variability that it has come to be thought of as unadventurous.

But, if the short story does not seem to be very popular with readers, it is still an essential part of the writing of fiction that offers its own satisfactions to the writer. The following stories certainly bear witness to its continued vitality and variety, and, I feel, to the various and particular satisfactions it can offer to the reader. Yet the short story cannot be infinitely variable; it has to be short and, whether it is a tale or a sketch, it has to be a *story*. It is in its quality as story that we can begin to get near to some understanding of it as a literary form rather than as simply an account of an event or a report of a surprising accident. If we think for a moment of the relation between a novel and a short story, then we can readily conceive of a novel as being different from or more than the story that supports it. We readily distinguish between plot and form and we are even tempted sometimes to discard the plot – what actually happens – as a mechanical contrivance, before we begin any serious discussion of what the novel is about. In the short story, on the other hand, there is only the story. There is time for nothing else, and the reader is drawn, quite without the ceremonies of an opening, into what is to happen. If we sometimes feel about a novel that it is finally an inflated short story, we are almost never inclined to think the reverse about a good short story. Good short stories would not have made better novels.

Perhaps in this distinction lies the continued attraction of the short story to the writer. In its unceremoniousness, its tight fit between story and meaning (and all the lessons in economy implied in saying that) lie a continuous challenge. A challenge also to the reader, since the good short story is not one that is simply realistic. All stories are constructions or inventions. Even where the movement of these stories appears inconsequential, the appearance is deceptive. Many of them revolve round or move towards the moment of arrival or departure, those moments which, in our lives, still have about them some trace of ritual when what we think and feel is quickened and heightened by a certain formality. Preparing for a first communion is the most obvious example of the kind of occasion I mean. But there are less obviously ritual moments, many of them involving initiation into the mysterious and complicated adult world, which are just as disturbing to the victim, more disturbing because unexpected and unprepared. A good half of these stories turn on this clash of the separate worlds of the child and the adult.

Again, as the comparison of any two or three of the stories included here would suggest, no two writers set about their subject in the same way. Each has his special idiom that, in its own way, persuades us readers to share this particular vision of the world constructed in this particular way. Each writer makes a different decision about the kind of narrating voice to be used and its place within or at a distance from the unfolding events. But it is not merely a trick of using a particular tone of voice that persuades us to share a writer's vision. Each voice is precisely located in a setting and all the stories here, no matter how diverse their idioms or their voices, do share the characteristic of taking place in a precisely defined location. It can be a near-deserted beach, wide open to the winds that blow from Russia, which seems to drain human existence of purpose and meaning. A ploughed, sloping field under the rain can strike us as equally threatening. A man swimming home from private pool to pool is so utterly distracted from life and purpose that he arrives to discover only waste and desolation. A loom shed constrains its inhabitants to endure a kind of hell on earth, pressing what life remains to them as human beings into startling shapes. The precise location of each story enfolds its author's vision of the world and captures the reader's attention. This is why I wrote that in the short story there is room for nothing but the story. If I see the form as endlessly variable, that is not the same as to say it is infinitely changeable. The close fit of story, location and vision imposes its own limitations on the freedom the author possesses. It is his task powerfully to exploit those limits. In this fashion the very precision demanded by the form exacts not only a very tight economy from the writer, but also imposes on him a reticence that, for the reader, becomes an accompanying, if silent, eloquence.

The precision leaves to be inferred much more than is stated, so that, if the event and its location have been precisely caught, the resulting vision works on the reader's mind in an echoing series of implications after the reading of the words is finished. Why, for example, is an ageing sponger's weakening fantasy of his place in the world assuaged and soothed by contemplating the animals at the zoo? Is our response to the story to feel that the author is tearing away our deceptions and self-deceptions, or that he is cautiously lifting the edge of those masks in order to persuade us that, without them, the pain of existence would be unendurable? Stripped of our fantasies and our absurd misunderstandings, would we be driven to act on impulse only, like the animals? Many questions surround the compulsion of a retired American college professor to elaborate a theology of good ducks and evil turtles. However, just as the writer's freedom is contained by the form, so the reader's questions are shaped by the directions at which the writer's reticence hints. Perhaps it was the case that the man who shot snapping turtles did use his academic knowledge of chemistry to kill off his rich relatives. Perhaps economic exploitation is the other face of his kind of moral absolutism as the ironic reversal of his story emphasizes. But what I mean by the implications of the writer's reticence for the reader's questioning is not covered by the relatively straightforward case of irony. Some of these stories are not ironic, although their concentration may sometimes make them appear to be so. Irony I take to be what Henry James once called 'the other possible case'; in other words, something we might have expected to happen but which did not. The other world at which the short story writer's enforced reticence hints is of another kind and is a product of formal concentration. I can best suggest what I mean by turning to the last story in this collection, which is a writer's own not altogether serious nightmare. At a first look, it is an attack on the outrageous idea that a computer could write a story, but it then reveals itself as a warning shot fired at those writers who surrender rather to formula than to form.

Looking over this collection as a whole, there seems to be no danger that the present vitality and variety of forms and voices could be reduced to a set of computerizable formulae. Collection seems to be not quite the right word to use here, for these stories contribute to neither a single theme nor to a single view of the world. Each is its own world of realization and implication, and each story seems to suggest that what we take the world to be reveals itself in the story we tell about it. That is what stories, or histories (in many languages it is the same word), have always told their readers.

Allan Grant

FRANK O'CONNOR

FRANK O'CONNOR (1903–66), pseudonym of Michael O'Donovan. Born in Cork. Largely self-educated. Primarily a short story writer, his first collection Guests of the Nation *came out in 1931. Other books included three about Ireland;* Art of the Theatre *(1947) (he was for a time Director of Dublin's Abbey Theatre); poetry; criticism, including* The Lonely Voice *(1963), a book about the short story; and autobiography.*

He gave all his stories an Irish setting, even when the germ for them came from elsewhere. His later years were spent out of Ireland, however, largely in his wife's native country, America.

First Confession

All the trouble began when my grandfather died and my grandmother – my father's mother – came to live with us. Relations in the one house are a strain at the best of times, but, to make matters worse, my grandmother was a real old countrywoman and quite unsuited to the life in town. She had a fat, wrinkled old face, and, to Mother's great indignation, went round the house in bare feet – the boots had her crippled, she said. For dinner she had a jug of porter and a pot of potatoes with – sometimes – a bit of salt fish, and she poured out the potatoes on the table and ate them slowly, with great relish, using her fingers by way of a fork.

Now, girls are supposed to be fastidious, but I was the one who suffered most from this. Nora, my sister, just sucked up to the old woman for the penny she got every Friday out of the old-age pension, a thing I could not do. I was too honest, that was my trouble; and when I was playing with Bill Connell, the sergeant-major's son, and saw my grandmother steering up the path with the jug of porter sticking out from beneath her shawl, I was mortified. I made excuses not to let him come into the house, because I could never be sure what she would be up to when we went in.

When Mother was at work and my grandmother made the dinner I wouldn't touch it. Nora once tried to make me, but I hid under the table from her and took the bread-knife with me for protection. Nora let on to be very indignant (she wasn't, of course, but she knew Mother saw through her, so she sided with Gran) and came after me. I lashed out at her with the bread-knife, and after that she left me alone. I stayed there till

Mother came in from work and made my dinner, but when Father came in later Nora said in a shocked voice: 'Oh, Dadda, do you know what Jackie did at dinner-time?' Then, of course, it all came out; Father gave me a flaking; Mother interfered, and for days after that he didn't speak to me and Mother barely spoke to Nora. And all because of that old woman! God knows, I was heart-scalded.

Then, to crown my misfortunes, I had to make my first confession and communion. It was an old woman called Ryan who prepared us for these. She was about the one age with Gran; she was well-to-do, lived in a big house on Montenotte, wore a black cloak and bonnet, and came every day to school at three o'clock when we should have been going home, and talked to us of hell. She may have mentioned the other place as well, but that could only have been by accident, for hell had the first place in her heart.

She lit a candle, took out a new half-crown, and offered it to the first boy who would hold one finger – only one finger! – in the flame for five minutes by the school clock. Being always very ambitious I was tempted to volunteer, but I thought it might look greedy. Then she asked were we afraid of holding one finger – only one finger! – in a little candle flame for five minutes and not afraid of burning all over in roasting hot furnaces for all eternity. 'All eternity! Just think of that! A whole lifetime goes by and it's nothing, not even a drop in the ocean of your sufferings.' The woman was really interesting about hell, but my attention was all fixed on the half-crown. At the end of the lesson she put it back in her purse. It was a great disappointment; a religious woman like that, you wouldn't think she'd bother about a thing like a half-crown.

Another day she said she knew a priest who woke one night to find a fellow he didn't recognize leaning over the end of his bed. The priest was a bit frightened – naturally enough – but he asked the fellow what he wanted, and the fellow said in a deep, husky voice that he wanted to go to confession. The

3

priest said it was an awkward time and wouldn't it do in the morning, but the fellow said that last time he went to confession, there was one sin he kept back, being ashamed to mention it, and now it was always on his mind. Then the priest knew it was a bad case, because the fellow was after making a bad confession and committing a mortal sin. He got up to dress, and just then the cock crew in the yard outside, and – lo and behold! – when the priest looked round there was no sign of the fellow, only a smell of burning timber, and when the priest looked at his bed didn't he see the print of two hands burned in it? That was because the fellow had made a bad confession. This story made a shocking impression on me.

But the worst of all was when she showed us how to examine our conscience. Did we take the name of the Lord, our God, in vain? Did we honour our father and our mother? (I asked her did this include grandmothers and she said it did.) Did we love our neighbours as ourselves? Did we covet our neighbour's goods? (I thought of the way I felt about the penny that Nora got every Friday.) I decided that, between one thing and another, I must have broken the whole ten commandments, all on account of that old woman, and so far as I could see, so long as she remained in the house I had no hope of ever doing anything else.

I was scared to death of confession. The day the whole class went I let on to have a toothache, hoping my absence wouldn't be noticed; but at three o'clock, just as I was feeling safe, along comes a chap with a message from Mrs Ryan that I was to go to confession myself on Saturday and be at the chapel for communion with the rest. To make it worse, Mother couldn't come with me and sent Nora instead.

Now, that girl had ways of tormenting me that Mother never knew of. She held my hand as we went down the hill, smiling sadly and saying how sorry she was for me, as if she were bringing me to the hospital for an operation.

'Oh, God help us!' she moaned. 'Isn't it a terrible pity you

4

weren't a good boy? Oh, Jackie, my heart bleeds for you! How will you ever think of all your sins? Don't forget you have to tell him about the time you kicked Gran on the shin.'

'Lemme go!' I said, trying to drag myself free of her. 'I don't want to go to confession at all.'

'But sure, you'll have to go to confession, Jackie,' she replied in the same regretful tone. 'Sure, if you didn't, the parish priest would be up to the house, looking for you. 'Tisn't, God knows, that I'm not sorry for you. Do you remember the time you tried to kill me with the bread-knife under the table? And the language you used to me? I don't know what he'll do with you at all, Jackie. He might have to send you up to the bishop.'

I remember thinking bitterly that she didn't know the half of what I had to tell – if I told it. I knew I couldn't tell it, and understood perfectly why the fellow in Mrs Ryan's story made a bad confession; it seemed to me a great shame that people wouldn't stop criticizing him. I remember that steep hill down to the church, and the sunlit hillsides beyond the valley of the river, which I saw in the gaps between the houses like Adam's last glimpse of Paradise.

Then, when she had manoeuvred me down the long flight of steps to the chapel yard, Nora suddenly changed her tone. She became the raging malicious devil she really was.

'There you are!' she said with a yelp of triumph, hurling me through the church door. 'And I hope he'll give you the penitential psalms, you dirty little caffler.'

I knew then I was lost, given up to eternal justice. The door with the coloured-glass panels swung shut behind me, the sunlight went out and gave place to deep shadow, and the wind whistled outside so that the silence within seemed to crackle like ice under my feet. Nora sat in front of me by the confession box. There were a couple of old women ahead of her, and then a miserable-looking poor devil came and wedged me in at the other side, so that I couldn't escape even if I had the courage. He joined his hands and rolled his eyes in the direction of the roof, muttering aspirations in an anguished tone, and I wondered had he a grandmother too. Only a grandmother could account for a fellow behaving in that heartbroken way, but he was better off than I, for he at least could go and confess his sins; while I would make a bad confession and then die in the night and be continually coming back and burning people's furniture.

Nora's turn came, and I heard the sound of something slamming, and then her voice as if butter wouldn't melt in her mouth, and then another slam, and out she came. God, the hypocrisy of women! Her eyes were lowered, her head was bowed, and her hands were joined very low down on her stomach, and she walked up the aisle to the side altar looking like a saint. You never saw such an exhibition of devotion; and I remembered the devilish malice with which she had tormented me all the way from our door, and wondered were all religious people like that, really. It was my turn now. With the fear of damnation in my soul I went in, and the confessional door closed of itself behind me.

It was pitch-dark and I couldn't see priest or anything else. Then I really began to be frightened. In the darkness it was a matter between God and me, and He had all the odds. He knew what my intentions were before I even started; I had no chance. All I had ever been told about confession got mixed up in my mind, and I knelt to one wall and said: 'Bless me, father, for I have sinned; this is my first confession.' I waited for a few minutes, but nothing happened, so I tried it on the other wall. Nothing happened there either. He had me spotted all right.

It must have been then that I noticed the shelf at about one height with my head. It was really a place for grown-up people to rest their elbows, but in my distracted state I thought it was probably the place you were supposed to kneel. Of course, it was on the high side and not very deep, but I was

6

always good at climbing and managed to get up all right. Staying up was the trouble. There was room only for my knees, and nothing you could get a grip on but a sort of wooden moulding a bit above it. I held on to the moulding and repeated the words a little louder, and this time something happened all right. A slide was slammed back; a little light entered the box, and a man's voice said: 'Who's there?'

''Tis me, father,' I said for fear he mightn't see me and go away again. I couldn't see him at all. The place the voice came from was under the moulding, about level with my knees, so I took a good grip of the moulding and swung myself down till I saw the astonished face of a young priest looking up at me. He had to put his head on one side to see me, and I had to put mine on one side to see him, so we were more or less talking to one another upside-down. It struck me as a queer way of hearing confessions, but I didn't feel it my place to criticize.

'Bless me, father, for I have sinned; this is my first confession,' I rattled off all in one breath, and swung myself down the least shade more to make it easier for him.

'What are you doing up there?' he shouted in an angry voice, and the strain the politeness was putting on my hold of the moulding, and the shock of being addressed in such an uncivil tone, were too much for me. I lost my grip, tumbled, and hit the door an unmerciful wallop before I found myself flat on my back in the middle of the aisle. The people who had been waiting stood up with their mouths open. The priest opened the door of the middle box and came out, pushing his biretta back from his forehead; he looked something terrible. Then Nora came scampering down the aisle.

'Oh, you dirty little caffler!' she said. 'I might have known you'd do it. I might have known you'd disgrace me. I can't leave you out of my sight for one minute.'

Before I could even get to my feet to defend myself she bent down and gave me a clip across the ear. This reminded me that I was so stunned I had even forgotten to cry, so that people might think I wasn't hurt at all, when in fact I was probably maimed for life. I gave a roar out of me.

'What's all this about?' the priest hissed, getting angrier than ever and pushing Nora off me. 'How dare you hit the child like that, you little vixen?'

'But I can't do my penance with him, father,' Nora cried, cocking an outraged eye up at him.

'Well, go and do it, or I'll give you some more to do,' he said, giving me a hand up. 'Was it coming to confession you were, my poor man?' he asked me.

''Twas, father,' said I with a sob.

'Oh,' he said respectfully, 'a big hefty fellow like you must have terrible sins. Is this your first?'

''Tis, father,' said I.

'Worse and worse,' he said gloomily. 'The crimes of a lifetime. I don't know will I get rid of you at all today. You'd better wait now till I'm finished with these old ones. You can see by the looks of them they haven't much to tell.'

'I will, father,' I said with something approaching joy.

The relief of it was really enormous. Nora stuck out her tongue at me from behind his back, but I couldn't even be bothered retorting. I knew from the very moment that man opened his mouth that he was intelligent above the ordinary. When I had time to think, I saw how right I was. It only stood to reason that a fellow confessing after seven years would have more to tell than people that went every week. The crimes of a lifetime, exactly as he said. It was only what he expected, and the rest was the cackle of old women and girls with their talk of hell, the bishop, and the penitential psalms. That was all they knew. I started to make my examination of conscience, and barring the one bad business of my grandmother it didn't seem so bad.

The next time, the priest steered me into the confession box himself and left the shutter back the way I could see him get in and sit down at the further side of the grille from me.

8

'Well, now,' he said, 'what do they call you?'

'Jackie, father,' said I.

'And what's a-trouble to you, Jackie?'

'Father,' I said, feeling I might as well get it over while I had him in good humour, 'I had it all arranged to kill my grandmother.'

He seemed a bit shaken by that, all right, because he said nothing for quite a while.

'My goodness,' he said at last, 'that'd be a shocking thing to do. What put that into your head?'

'Father,' I said, feeling very sorry for myself, 'she's an awful woman.'

'Is she?' he asked. 'What way is she awful?'

'She takes porter, father,' I said, knowing well from the way Mother talked of it that this was a mortal sin, and hoping it would make the priest take a more favourable view of my case.

'Oh, my!' he said, and I could see he was impressed.

'And snuff, father,' said I.

'That's a bad case, sure enough, Jackie,' he said.

'And she goes round in her bare feet, father,' I went on in a rush of self-pity, 'and she know I don't like her, and she gives pennies to Nora and none to me, and my da sides with her and flakes me, and one night I was so heart-scalded I made up my mind I'd have to kill her.'

'And what would you do with the body?' he asked with great interest.

'I was thinking I could chop that up and carry it away in a barrow I have,' I said.

'Begor, Jackie,' he said, 'do you know you're a terrible child?'

'I know, father,' I said, for I was just thinking the same thing myself. 'I tried to kill Nora too with a bread-knife under the table, only I missed her.'

'Is that the little girl that was beating you just now?' he asked.

"'Tis, father.'

'Someone will go for her with a bread-knife one day, and he won't miss her,' he said rather cryptically. 'You must have great courage. Between ourselves, there's a lot of people I'd like to do the same to but I'd never have the nerve. Hanging is an awful death.'

'Is it, father?' I asked with the deepest interest – I was always very keen on hanging. 'Did you ever see a fellow hanged?'

'Dozens of them,' he said solemnly. 'And they all died roaring.'

'Jay!' I said.

'Oh, a horrible death!' he said with great satisfaction. 'Lots of the fellows I saw killed their grandmothers too, but they all said 'twas never worth it.'

He had me there fore a full ten minutes talking, and then walked out the chapel yard with me. I was genuinely sorry to part with him, because he was the most entertaining character I'd ever met in the religious line. Outside, after the shadow of the church, the sunlight was like the roaring of waves on a beach; it dazzled me; and when the frozen silence melted and I heard the screech of trams on the road my heart soared. I knew now I wouldn't die in the night and come back, leaving marks on my mother's furniture. It would be a great worry to her, and the poor soul had enough.

Nora was sitting on the railing, waiting for me, and she put on a very sour puss when she saw the priest with me. She was mad jealous because a priest had never come out of the church with her.

'Well,' she asked coldly, after he left me, 'what did he give you?'

'Three Hail Marys,' I said.

'Three Hail Marys,' she repeated incredulously. 'You mustn't have told him anything.'

'I told him everything,' I said confidently.

'About Gran and all?'

'About Gran and all.'

(All she wanted was to be able to go home and say I'd made a bad confession.)

'Did you tell him you went for me with the bread-knife?' she asked with a frown.

'I did to be sure.'

'And he only gave you three Hail Marys?'

'That's all.'

She slowly got down from the railing with a baffled air. Clearly, this was beyond her. As we mounted the steps back to the main road she looked at me suspiciously.

'What are you sucking?' she asked.

'Bullseyes.'

'Was it the priest gave them to you?'

''Twas.'

'Lord God,' she wailed bitterly, 'some people have all the luck! 'Tis no advantage to anybody trying to be good. I might just as well be a sinner like you.'

FRANK SARGESON

FRANK SARGESON (1903–   ) Born in New Zealand, where he has lived all his life; variously a solicitor, civil servant and market gardener. He has written novels, but is primarily a short story writer. His hallmark seems to be a kind of direct speech in which the authentic New Zealand voice is heard.

Chaucerian

When I was a young man I used to go to the Unitarian Church. In those days it was the thing for quite a number of young men to go to the Unitarian Church. It was their way of letting people know they had grown up and had independent minds. These days I think it is the thing for young men who want to let people know that they have grown up and have independent minds to join the Communist Party.

Well, I went to the Unitarian Church. As far as I could make out about a dozen other people went there too. Sometimes there were less. There was something wrong somewhere. I couldn't make out just what it was.

Then one lunch hour I went for a walk in Freeman's Bay. In case you don't know I'd better say that Freeman's Bay is that part of Auckland over beyond Hobson Street. It's a very interesting place. Any New Zealand poet who hasn't absolutely dedicated himself to kauri trees and bell-birds couldn't do better than go and live there.

As I was saying, I went for a walk one lunch hour in Freeman's Bay and I saw a big navvy with bowyangs tied round his trouser-legs. He was striding along hand in hand with his little girl, and the little girl had to run to keep up with him; and the next moment they both disappeared into the bar of a pub. I was shocked. You wouldn't blame me for that if you knew how strict my parents were. I didn't know a thing for all that I was letting people know that I had grown up and had an independent mind by going to the Unitarian Church. From where I stood I could see inside the bar and I saw the barman pump up some beer and put it in front of the navvy. The little girl had a rag doll under her arm, and after she had stood on her toes and tried to look over the bar she came out to the door and tried to make the rag doll sit on the door-knob.

Now I admit that in those days I didn't know a thing. My parents had been too strict. But I had read a few books, and I was fond of reading Chaucer's Canterbury Tales. Well, as I stood there watching the little girl trying to make her rag doll sit on the door-knob all my confusion about myself and about the Unitarian Church suddenly left me. I got the idea that what I was looking at was about as near as I'd ever get to the Canterbury Tales outside the covers of a book. I'm not quite clear about how I got inside that bar but I did get in. And I drank two half-handles with the navvy. Sure enough he told me things that might have come out of the Canterbury Tales. And he called me mate. The little girl showed me her doll. It was called Humpty Dumpty and could have done with a dry clean.

Well, it all happened a long time ago; and it's a long story. The navvy and his wife were looking for a boarder.

As I say it all happened a long time ago. The little girl is grown up now, and she's got a mind that's a good deal more independent than mine is. A moment ago she looked over my shoulder and said, 'You big silly, what do you want to write about that for?'

I'm glad I didn't marry that Mabel Tittering who was so good at playing Winking at the only Unitarian Church social I ever went to.

DAN JACOBSON

DAN JACOBSON (1929–   ) Born in Johannesburg, educated at the University of Witwatersrand. Worked as a teacher, a journalist and on an Israeli kibbutz. His first novel The Trap *(1955) illuminates colour prejudices, a theme he came back to in* The Price of Diamonds *(1957) and* The Evidence of Love *(1960). He now lives in London. He has in two recent novels,* The Beginners *(1966) and* The Rape of Tamar *(1970), moved away from this preoccupation. 'The Boss' comes from a collection of short stories,* Beggar My Neighbour, *published in 1964. His most recent novel is* The Wonder Worker *(1974).*

The Boss

'And this,' Mr Kramer said to Miss Posen, 'is my son, Lionel.'

'Mr Kramer! You're teasing me,' Miss Posen said reprovingly.

The old man winked at his son, who stood with him at Miss Posen's desk. Embarrassed but proud, determined not to reveal the quiver within him, Lionel turned to go to the next room, but his father took him by the sleeve. 'You must let Miss Posen have a good look, so that she'll remember you.'

'Oh, Mr Kramer!'

And the young man said: 'Miss Posen's seen me often enough.'

'But you are different now. We are all different aren't we, Lily, now that the younger generation has come to take our place?'

The boy was smiling, flattered but a little wearied by his father's pleasure in him. 'I'm no different from what I was. And we're interfering with Miss Posen's work.'

'Do you hear that?' Mr Kramer jokingly shook his finger at Miss Posen. 'Already Lionel is worrying about the work. It's a good sign, Lily. We'll all have to work hard now that he is here. New hands and a new young man make a new order.'

It seemed that Miss Posen could respond only by shaking her head and blushing slightly. But she managed to say: 'You're young enough, Mr Kramer—' She shook her head again.

'How can you say that, when the proof is standing here next to me that one of these days I must go?' The old man spoke mischievously, provoking them both.

'I don't believe it,' Miss Posen said, looking down at the papers on her desk.

There was a sudden pause. Frightened at the effect of her words Miss Posen said: 'All I can do is to carry on with my work. That's all you want of me, Mr Kramer?'

'Of course.'

'Come, Dad.'

'I'm coming, I'm coming.' And the old man followed his son, who was already half-way down the office. But at the door he turned and said to Miss Posen, smiling as he spoke, 'You see, already he is giving me orders.'

To Lionel Mr Kramer said, in his own office, 'Poor girl. Did you see how red she went?' Screwing up his face he scratched at his cheek several times, with the back of his nails, roughly almost contemptuously. 'On her cheeks here,' he said. 'You'd think she was still seventeen.'

'She's a long way from seventeen,' the son said, who was eighteen. He was sitting in the chair in front of the desk.

'A long way,' the father agreed. 'Poor girl!' Miss Posen was over forty, but Mr Kramer almost invariably referred to her with scorn and affection as a 'poor girl' – she was so plain and dull, and would never get married. Because he had come to South Africa as an immigrant boy and was now entirely through his own efforts the manager of a large butter factory, he could afford to be scornful of failures like Lily Posen. But he reminded his son, 'It's a long time she's been here, yet she still does a good day's work, she doesn't let up.'

'I know, I know. You talk as if I'm a stranger here. Christ, I grew up in the factory – I've always been here. What is this nonsense of yours? – introducing me to Miss Posen and all the others in the office. It just makes me look ridiculous.'

'You don't have to worry about that. You don't look ridiculous to them so easily.'

'You don't understand.'

'No—?' the father asked, his eyes moving sharply towards his son. But he restrained himself. 'And now for some tea.'

'When do I start work?'

'After tea.' Mr Kramer pressed the bell on his desk, and when a girl came in he asked, 'How about some tea, Betty? Two cups, please.'

The father was the first to speak after she had left the office. 'So you don't think you'll regret it, now that you've seen it all?'

'I've told you, Dad, I've seen it a thousand times.'

'With a difference. Now it isn't a matter of coming here for a few weeks in your school holidays, or for an afternoon when you've been to town with some friends. Now it's every day, every morning – the same things, the same work, the same people. . . . You won't be jealous when your friends come from the university and tell you what a good time they're having there?'

'I won't be jealous. We've been over all this before. I don't want to go to the university.' Lionel's voice was querulous. He was tall, tanned, with a lean face and large brown eyes – physically unlike his father, but with something of his father's shrugging movements in his shoulders. 'I'm not interested in wasting my time. And your money. I'm here, I know what I'm doing.'

They waited in silence for the tea to come in. When it did Lionel drank his quickly, put the cup back on the tray, and stood up. 'I'm starting work now.'

'Ask Barton to show you the accounts. Your first job is to learn some names.'

At the door Lionel turned; he pushed the door to and fro in his hand for a moment. 'You'll see, Dad. You'll be able to depend on me. I'm not scared of responsibility.'

'That's what I want, Lionel. I'm getting to be an old man, and I think I'll be glad to rely on you.' Seeing the slight trim figure of his son, standing there half-defiant and half-afraid in his brown business suit, the old man's heart moved with pride and pain in his breast.

Often Mr Kramer sat lazily in his office in the mornings, drinking tea, reading the papers and the correspondence that came in, studying – out of an unceasing curiosity and respect for the things of this world – the advertisements for goods he would never buy. But on Lionel's first day at work he was up and about all day. Squat, his skull shining, his shoulders broad, he walked about eagerly and authoritatively, one hand flying up to acknowledge an employee's greeting: he went backwards and forwards between the office block and the factory, at ease and in command in both. For his employees he had a hasty paternal regard; he was easy with them, for he knew they were dependent on him.

He went with Lionel, or he followed Lionel and spoke to those Lionel had just spoken to, or he merely watched; and by the end of the day he was able to say to Miss Posen, 'The boy is shaping well. Soon Lionel will really be ordering me around.'

'No, Mr Kramer.'

Curiously, humorously, Mr Kramer watched her. 'You think not, Lily?'

'No one has ever told you what to do, not as long as I've been here. And you know how long that is, Mr Kramer.'

'Everything begins, and everything ends, sooner or later.'

'No, Mr Kramer,' Miss Posen said, daring to insist. And as a reward he gave her a lift home that evening.

Before Lionel had come to work in the firm, when he had been a schoolboy, all the white employees had called him Lionel; now that he was working in a position of authority among them, they called him Mr Lionel. All but Miss Posen. She presumed on the fact that she was the oldest employee, both in age and in years of service; and she continued to call him Lionel. She presumed too – Lionel secretly was sure – on the fact that she was the only Jewish employee, and he hated the last presumption even more than he did the others, for it seemed to drag him down to a level where he was forever equal with her.

After a few weeks he complained to his father. 'No one else calls me just Lionel. Why should she? It sets a bad example to everyone else in the office.'

'Yes,' Mr Kramer agreed.

'She tries to pretend that I don't matter around here, that I'm still a little boy.'

'Then you must show her that you're not.'

Lionel had hoped that somehow his father might do that for him, but now he had no choice in the matter. A few days passed before he could bring himself to do it, but in the end he did call Miss Posen into his father's office, and in his father's presence he told her that he wanted her to call him Mr Lionel. His courage almost failed him, and he wheedled her: 'I know it's hard for you, because you've been here for so long, and can remember me when I was just a little boy, but so can others on the staff. I have that against me, and I want you to set an example to them.'

Miss Posen moved her hands, clasped in front of her bosom, uneasily within one another. She was heavily built and bespectacled; her glasses were tinged faintly blue, and she usually wore blue dresses and blue jumpers – 'to match'. Mr Kramer had once said, 'her glasses'. She had been so long in the office that she could do any work she was asked to do: typing, sending out accounts and farmers' cheques, supervising the work of the other girls, a certain amount of book-keeping. But for all the slowness of her movements and the heaviness of her figure, the years as they passed had done nothing to wear out of her a kind of girlishness that could as easily find expression in a blush and a giggle of excitement as in a silly settled obstinacy.

Now she stood dumb in the office, blushing faintly. Her blue glasses sought for instruction from Mr Kramer's gaze. But the old man stared to one side, as if unconscious of the plea.

'I wouldn't mind you calling me whatever you like when we're alone like this,' Lionel said, wheedling again. 'But in the office, with the others there – I'd be glad of your co-operation.' The last phrase sounded so business-like he was able to bring it out briskly.

'It's difficult for me to remember,' Miss Posen said with a start. Her voice was uncertain – she was still looking for support or even response from Lionel's father. There was none; and she seemed to give in, to surrender. 'I will try, Lionel. I suppose – that – I've been here so long. . . . I can remember when you used to come to me for sweets.'

'That's over now.'

'I suppose it is – if you want—'

'I've told you what I want.'

Lionel got to his feet, and opened the door for her, as a consolation, and she went out with a last look back, in time to see Mr Kramer pulling hard but still absently at his cheek with the thumb and forefinger of one hand.

Lionel felt virtuous, having done what he had. 'That settles that,' he said to his father.

But that had not settled that. For Miss Posen continued to call Lionel just Lionel. The first few times it happened Lionel told himself that it was merely a slip on her part. But she persisted. She called him Lionel as if she couldn't imagine calling him anything else, as if he had never spoken to her.

Eventually Lionel complained to his father again. 'She's sly. She pretends she doesn't know what she's doing, but she knows well enough. She's doing it on purpose. She wants to drag me down.'

'Why should she want to do that?'

'You know why,' Lionel said bluntly. 'It's obvious – I don't know why you pretend that you don't. She's old and finished and she's got it against me because I'm young and on top of her.'

Mr Kramer shrugged his shoulders. 'Speak to her again, if you're so cross.'

This time Lionel spoke privately to Miss Posen, less wheedlingly and more harshly; and again she promised that she would mend her ways. An hour later she called him Lionel. And not only did she continue to call him just Lionel; she became, as Lionel described it to his father, 'cheeky'. Still heavy, reluctant, hard-working, she nevertheless was cheeky as well – and cheeky publicly, cheeky in front of other members of the staff, cheeky even in front of Lionel's father. 'You'll do this for me, won't you Miss Posen?' Lionel might say, and she'd simply say, 'No.' Or he'd say, 'Get that file for me, Miss Posen', and she, with her eyes downcast, her voice low, would answer, 'Get it yourself.'

Lionel could hardly believe his ears, when she spoke to him like this. He went pale, under his tanned skin; his dark eyes stared forward: then he would move, he would do the job himself, working brusquely, pretending to be concerned only with the business in hand. And though the others in the office were wary after each incident, once the shock had passed they wondered, Lionel was sure, what they too might one day be able to get away with.

'You've heard the way she talks to me,' Lionel said to his father. 'It's impossible, things can't go on like this. You've got to do something with her, Dad.'

'If I bring her in here, and speak to her severely, certainly she'll stop being cheeky to you. But it will be because of me, not because of you. She'll think less of you, and so will everyone else in the office when they hear of it. They will think that Mr Lionel can't look after himself, that he has to come running to his father like a little boy. Is that what you want them to think of you?'

'If you really wanted to help me, you'd find a way to do it.'

'Lionel, this is a battle, it's your first battle. You must win it by yourself, or you won't have confidence when the next one comes. And who are you fighting against, after all? Only that poor girl, Lily Posen, who sits like dough in the office. Can't you get the better of her?'

'You're on her side!' Lionel shouted suddenly.

Mr Kramer seemed undisturbed by the accusation. Smiling, his eyes half-closed, he said, 'Lionel, I am on my side. That's what I'm trying to teach you to be for yourself.'

'All right,' Lionel warned his father, 'you'll see. I'll fix this business by myself. And then you'll know too.'

So Lionel watched Miss Posen, watching for his opportunity. No one had ever watched her before; and Lionel was rewarded when for the first time he opened her handbag in the secrecy of the lavatory and found in it a small roll of penny stamps. The stamps might have been her own, but he was sure they were not. He did not say anything about it at the time – he merely made a note of the date, and the amount of the stamps, and returned the bag to its place on her desk. Then whenever he could – when she was out on some message to the factory and there was no one else in her office – he opened her bag to see what he could find. He found a typewriter-ribbon in a still-sealed tin; he found erasers; a box of paper-clips, a rubber thimble, a ball-point pen. All of these things he put back in her bag, making a note of what each had been, and the date on which he had found it. Soon he had a little dossier on Miss Posen's pilfering; he looked back with pride to the day he had noticed that certain items of stationery were disappearing faster than they should have been from the stationery-cabinet – to which Miss Posen, as the oldest employee, had a key. And he looked forward with resolution to the day when he would confront her with what she had done.

One morning Lionel went into the office that she shared with another girl; Miss Posen was standing at the filing-cabinet, going through some papers. Lionel asked her: 'Have you got the figures I wanted yesterday?'

'No.'

'When will you have them?'

'When they're ready, Lionel.' She went on with the sorting of her papers.

'When will that be?' Lionel's voice was loud with anger.

Hers was low. 'Say the bells of Stepney.'

Lionel knew that his father would be out of the office that afternoon.

'I'll speak to you later,' he said. 'Come into my father's office at three o'clock.'

At three o'clock he was seated at his father's desk with the sheet of paper containing her record on the table in front of him. When she came in, he spoke without looking up, hardly opening his mouth, so that his voice would not tremble. 'Miss Posen, I have something very important to speak to you about.' He did not invite her to sit down. 'On the twelfth of October you took from this office penny stamps to the value of one shilling. On the seventeenth of October you took a box of paper-clips. On the eighteenth, an unused pencil. On the first of November, three pencils. . . .' And so he went on, down the list. He forced himself to look up when he had finished. 'What have you got to say about that? You've been stealing from us.'

When he saw her – so old, so dull, her shoulders hanging uselessly in her blue dress – Lionel's fear left him, and so too did his shame. He could stare hard at her, he could shout at her if he wanted to. Suddenly he knew his own power, and he was enraged. 'You're a thief! My father has employed you for fifteen years, and you repay everything he's done for you by stealing from him! What are you without him? Nothing! Nothing! And you steal from him!'

Miss Posen did not burst into tears, as he was expecting her to. She turned and almost ran out of the office. The heavy, fugitive, graceless scuttle fed his rage with her again.

When his father came back from town he told him what had happened. 'She's got to go,' Lionel shouted. 'I've found

her out and she's got to go. I've shown who I am now!' He
was pale, his hand was trembling, but his eyes were bright, and
Mr Kramer could see that he had tasted blood, that he was
exulting in his own power.

Between his son and Miss Posen Mr Kramer did not have a
moment's hesitation as to which he should choose. One of the
two had to go now, and it would not be his son. But it was for
his own position too that the old man knew he had to fight.

So he listened to Lionel, and when Lionel had exhausted
himself and had slumped suddenly into a chair, Mr Kramer
said quietly, 'Now I want to speak to Miss Posen.' When
Lionel sat where he was Mr Kramer said, 'I want to speak
to her alone. I want to find out the truth of what has been
happening.'

'The truth! What do you mean?'

Mr Kramer ignored the protest. 'Tell Miss Posen that I
want to see her, and then go and make yourself busy somewhere.'

Miss Posen broke down when Mr Kramer said gently to her,
'It was a foolish thing for you to do, Lily.' Miss Posen wept; the
tears stole down under her blue glasses, and she lifted them to
wipe the tears away, showing Mr Kramer a glimpse of two
large, wet, naked eyes. But even before she had finished drying
her eyes, Mr Kramer had haltingly begun to explain why he
could not give her another chance.

'I would, Lily,' he said. 'You've been working for me for
fifteen years, and that means something to me. But I can't.'

'Please, Mr Kramer – please help me. I don't know why I've
been taking these things – I haven't been doing it for long—'

'I know. Ever since Lionel's been here.'

Miss Posen was silenced; she stood stiff, as if shocked at
what he had said. Seeing this Mr Kramer explained: 'I know
how long you've been doing it, not because I've been watching
you, Lily, but because I know how these things are. Shouldn't

I know? Shouldn't I know better than anyone else in the world how you are feeling? Am I not in the same position? And that's why I can't give you another chance, Lily. It's that boy, that Lionel. You see how fierce he is. He's a youngster, but I can't go against him. I'm not strong enough. I'm telling you this, Lily, because you've been with me for fifteen years – to anyone else I wouldn't tell such a thing, I'd be too ashamed.' He spoke so haltingly and with such small shrugs of his shoulders, with such a downcast head, that Miss Posen almost tried to comfort him. But he would not accept her comfort. 'It's what I told you the first day he was here,' he said. 'My time is finished.'

Later he promised her that he would see to it that she got another position with some other firm in town, just as good a position as the one she was leaving. 'I know it will not be the same,' he said, 'but it is the best that I can do, with that boy here. And I will do it. We'll say that you're leaving because you and Lionel couldn't get on well together, and that's the only reason. Lionel will keep his mouth closed, he's the kind of strong boy who can.'

When she left the office, Miss Posen passed Lionel in the corridor outside. As a result of Mr Kramer's words she had recovered sufficiently to say fiercely to him, 'You're a dirty little boy!' Suddenly bright red and pale blue she exclaimed, 'You should be ashamed of yourself!'

Lionel came sideways into his father's office, looking back. 'You hear what she said?' He was amazed that she should have turned on him.

'Yes, I heard,' Mr Kramer said, with no expression in his voice. 'I've done it,' he told Lionel. 'You can be happy now. She's going, I've told her to get out, poor girl, and she won't be worrying you any longer.'

'It isn't just that she was worrying me! She was stealing!'

'Miss Posen! If I had known she was taking such things, such rubbish, like pencils and stamps, after fifteen years of

work, I would have turned my head away. I could never have
done what you did – watching, planning, setting traps, looking
into the poor girl's handbag. Miss Posen's! I would have been
ashamed. And then dragging the poor girl into the office and
having such a scene with her. . . .'

'Wasn't I right?' Lionel demanded. 'Didn't I find out about
her?'

'By your lights, perhaps, you were right. Your lights seem
to be different from mine, that's all. I'm just a man who wants
peace and kindness, and who thinks that a woman has worked
fifteen years . . . fifteen years! It is nearly as long as you have
been alive.'

'But—'

'But you did what you thought was right. I know. I can see
that. And perhaps you were right, but it isn't my way of being
right. And now I've got the problem of finding a place for her
just as good as the one she held here. It's the very least I can
do for the poor girl, after what has happened here. Fifteen
years! It's her lifetime that's passed here, and what have you
given her to show for it? Ach,' the old man said, 'it's no good
to think of it.'

Mr Kramer was as good as his word in getting Miss Posen a
new position.He also bought her an expensive farewell present,
and gave her a small party on her last afternoon in the office.
At the party Lionel heard Miss Posen describe Mr Kramer as
the best man she had ever known. Lionel did not know what
was happening to him.

His father did nothing to enlighten him. When Lionel
wanted to talk of it, all he heard from his father was, 'You did
what you thought was right. Poor Miss Posen! Poor girl! And
her father a little tailor! But perhaps a hard heart is a good
thing to have in business nowadays, though I managed without one.'

'I haven't a hard heart,' Lionel pleaded with his father.
'Dad, I did what I thought was *right*.'

'You did it, and that was enough. Now it's over and done with and forgotten. Except by that poor Miss Posen. She'll remember, it will be like a scar on her heart, all her life.'

'Please, Dad, listen to me—'

'Who doesn't listen to you now?' Mr Kramer asked, his arms wide open, his face lifted in surprise.

'You don't,' Lionel said.

'What? Didn't I throw that poor girl out after fifteen years, push her out like she was nothing to me, because you told me to?'

'You did, I know. Oh,' Lionel said miserably, 'I don't know.'

'What don't you know?'

It was hard for Lionel to make the admission. 'Anything at all.'

Mr Kramer knew he had won his fight. 'You'll learn,' he said.

The tenderness in his voice made Lionel wonder, but to that too he had to submit.

PATRICK WHITE

PATRICK WHITE (1912–) Australian novelist, though born in England and educated at Cheltenham and King's College, Cambridge. He settled in London and his first novel Happy Valley *was published there in 1939. Served as an RAF Intelligence Officer during the Second World War. He has published many novels, probably the best-known being* Voss *(1957); the latest is* The Eye of the Storm *(1973); also a volume of plays and a collection of short stories* (The Burnt Ones, *1964) from which 'Willy-Wagtails by Moonlight' is taken. His principal reputation is as a novelist and that reputation has grown steadily. In his novels he deals with the major themes of good and evil, and with man's quest for spiritual significance.*

Patrick White returned to Australia in 1948 and now lives near Sydney.

In 1973 he was awarded the Nobel Prize for Literature.

Willy-Wagtails by Moonlight

The Wheelers drove up to the Mackenzies' punctually at six-thirty. It was the hour for which they had been asked. My God, thought Jum Wheeler. It had been raining a little, and the tyres sounded blander on the wet gravel.

In front of the Mackenzies', which was what is known as a Lovely Old Home – colonial style – amongst some carefully natural-looking gums, there stood a taxi.

'Never knew Arch and Nora ask us with anyone else,' Eileen Wheeler said.

'Maybe they didn't. Even now. Maybe it's someone they couldn't get rid of.'

'Or an urgent prescription from the chemist's.'

Eileen Wheeler yawned. She must remember to show sympathy, because Nora Mackenzie was going through a particularly difficult one.

Anyway, they were there, and the door stood open on the lights inside. Even the lives of the people you know, even the lives of Nora and Arch look interesting for a split second, when you drive up and glimpse them through a lit doorway.

'It's that Miss Cullen,' Eileen said.

For there was Miss Cullen, doing something with a brief-case in the hall.

'Ugly bitch,' Jum said.

'Plain is the word,' corrected Eileen.

'Arch couldn't do without her. Practically runs the business.'

Certainly that Miss Cullen looked most methodical, shuffling the immaculate papers, and slipping them into a new pigskin brief-case in Arch and Nora's hall.

'Got a figure,' Eileen conceded.

'But not a chin.'

'Oh, hello, Miss Cullen. It's stopped raining.'

It was too bright stepping suddenly into the hall. The Wheelers brightly blinked. They looked newly made.

'Keeping well, Miss Cullen, I hope?'

'I have nothing to complain about, Mr Wheeler,' Miss Cullen replied.

She snapped the catch. Small, rather pointed breasts under the rain-coat. But, definitely, no chin.

Eileen Wheeler was fixing her hair in the reproduction Sheraton mirror.

She had been to the hairdresser's recently, and the do was still set too tight.

'Well, good-bye now,' Miss Cullen said.

When she smiled there was a hint of gold, but discreet, no more than a bridge. Then she would draw her lips together, and lick them ever so slightly, as if she had been sucking a not unpleasantly acid sweetie.

Miss Cullen went out the door, closing it firmly but quietly behind her.

'That was Miss Cullen,' said Nora Mackenzie coming down. 'She's Arch's secretary.'

'He couldn't do without her,' she added, as though they did not know.

Nora was like that. Eileen wondered how she and Nora had tagged along together, ever since Goulburn, all those years.

'God, she's plain!' Jum said.

Nora did not exactly frown, but pleated her forehead the way she did when other people's virtues were assailed. Such attacks seemed to affect her personally, causing her almost physical pain.

'But Mildred is so kind,' she insisted.

Nora Mackenzie made a point of calling her husband's

employees by first names, trying to make them part of a family which she alone, perhaps, would have liked to exist.

'She brought me some giblet soup, all the way from Balgowlah, that time I had virus 'flu.'

'Was it good, darling?' Eileen asked.

She was going through the routine, rubbing Nora's cheek with her own. Nora was pale. She must remember to be kind.

Nora did not answer, but led the way into the lounge-room.

Nora said:

'I don't think I'll turn on the lights for the present. They hurt my eyes, and it's so restful sitting in the dusk.'

Nora *was* pale. She had, in fact, just taken a couple of Disprin.

'Out of sorts, dear?' Eileen asked.

Nora did not answer, but offered some dry martinis.

Very watery, Jum knew from experience, but drink of a kind.

'Arch will be down presently,' Nora said. 'He had to attend to some business, some letters Miss Cullen brought. Then he went in to have a shower.'

Nora's hands were trembling as she offered the dry martinis, but Eileen remembered they always had.

The Wheelers sat down. It was all so familiar, they did not have to be asked, which was fortunate, as Nora Mackenzie always experienced difficulty in settling guests into chairs. Now she sat down herself, far more diffidently than her friends. The cushions were standing on their points.

Eileen sighed. Old friendships and the first scent of gin always made her nostalgic.

'It's stopped raining,' she said, and sighed.

'Arch well?' Jum asked.

As if he cared. She had let the ice get into the cocktail, turning it almost to pure water.

'He has his trouble,' Nora said. 'You know, his back.'

Daring them to have forgotten.

Nora loved Arch. It made Eileen feel ashamed.

So fortunate for them to have discovered each other. Nora Leadbeatter and Arch Mackenzie. Two such bores. And with bird-watching in common. Though Eileen Wheeler had never believed Nora did not make herself learn to like watching birds.

At Goulburn, in the early days, Nora would come out to Glen Davie sometimes to be with Eileen at week-ends. Mr Leadbeatter had been manager at the Wales for a while. He always saw that his daughter had the cleanest notes. Nora was shy, but better than nothing, and the two girls would sit about on the veranda those summer evenings, buffing their nails, and listening to the sheep cough in the home paddock. Eileen gave Nora lessons in making-up. Nora had protested, but was pleased.

'Mother well, darling?' Eileen asked, sipping that sad, watery gin.

'Not exactly *well*,' Nora replied, painfully.

Because she had been to Orange, to visit her widowed mother, who suffered from Parkinson's disease.

'You know what I mean, dear,' said Eileen.

Jum was dropping his ash on the carpet. It might be better when poor bloody Arch came down.

'I have an idea that woman, that Mrs Galloway, is unkind to her,' Nora said.

'Get another,' Eileen advised. 'It isn't like after the War.'

'One can never be sure,' Nora debated. 'One would hate to hurt the woman's feelings.'

Seated in the dusk Nora Mackenzie was of a moth colour. Her face looked as though she had been rubbing it with chalk. Might have, too, in spite of those lessons in make-up. She sat and twisted her hands together.

How very red Nora's hands had been, at Goulburn, at the convent, to which the two girls had gone. Not that they belonged to *those*. It was only convenient. Nora's hands had been red and trembly after practising a tarantella, early, in the frost. So very early all of that. Eileen had learnt about life shortly after puberty. She had tried to tell Nora one or two things, but Nora did not want to hear. Oh, no, no, *please*, Eileen, Nora cried. As though a boy had been twisting her arm. She had those long, entreating, sensitive hands.

And there they were still. Twisting together, making their excuses. For what they had never done.

Arch came in then. He turned on the lights, which made Nora wince, even those lights which barely existed in all the neutrality of Nora's room. Nora did not comment, but smiled, because it was Arch who had committed the crime.

Arch said:

'You two toping hard as usual.'

He poured himself the rest of the cocktail.

Eileen laughed her laugh which people found amusing at parties.

Jum said, and bent his leg, if it hadn't been for Arch and the shower, they wouldn't have had the one too many.

'A little alcohol releases the vitality,' Nora remarked ever so gently.

She always grew anxious at the point where jokes became personal.

Arch composed his mouth under the handle-bars moustache, and Jum knew what they were in for.

'Miss Cullen came out with one or two letters,' Arch was taking pains to explain. 'Something she thought should go off tonight. I take a shower most evenings. Summer, at least.'

'Such humidity,' Nora helped.

Arch looked down into his glass. He might have been composing further remarks, but did not come out with them.

That silly, bloody English-air-force-officer's moustache. It was the only thing Arch had ever dared. War had given him the courage to pinch a detail which did not belong to him.

'That Miss Cullen, useful girl,' Jum suggested.

'Runs the office.'

'Forty, if a day,' Eileen said, whose figure was beginning to slacken off.

Arch said he would not know, and Jum made a joke about Miss Cullen's *cul-de-sac*.

The little pleats had appeared again in Nora Mackenzie's chalky brow. 'Well,' she cried, jumping up, quite girlish, 'I do hope the dinner will be a success.'

And laughed.

Nora was half-way through her second course with that woman at the Chanticleer. Eileen suspected there would be avocadoes stuffed with prawns, chicken *Mornay*, and *crêpes Suzette*.

Eileen was right.

Arch seemed to gain in authority sitting at the head of his table.

'I'd like you to taste this wine,' he said. 'It's very light.'

'Oh, yes?' said Jum.

The wine was corked, but nobody remarked. The second bottle, later on, was somewhat better. The Mackenzies were spreading themselves tonight.

Arch flipped his napkin once or twice, emphasizing a point. He smoothed the handle-bars moustache, which should have concealed a harelip, only there wasn't one. Jum dated from before the moustache, long, long, very long.

Arch said:

'There was a story Armitage told me at lunch. There was a man who bought a mower. Who suffered from indigestion. Now, how, exactly, did it . . . go?'

Jum had begun to make those little pellets out of bread. It always fascinated him how grubby the little pellets turned out. And himself not by any means dirty.

Arch failed to remember the point of the story Armitage had told.

It was difficult to understand how Arch had made a success

of his business. Perhaps it was that Miss Cullen, breasts and all, under the rain-coat. For a long time Arch had messed around. Travelled in something. Separator parts. Got the agency for some sort of phoney machine for supplying *ozone* to public buildings. The Mackenzies lived at Burwood then. Arch continued to mess around. The War was quite a godsend. Arch was the real adje type. Did a conscientious job. Careful with his allowances, too.

Then, suddenly, after the War, Arch Mackenzie had launched out, started the import-export business. Funny the way a man will suddenly hit on the idea to which his particular brand of stupidity can respond.

The Mackenzies had moved to the North Shore, to the house which still occasionally embarrassed Nora. She felt as though she ought to apologize for success. But there was the bird-watching. Most week-ends they went off to the bush, to the Mountains or somewhere. She felt happier in humbler circumstances. In time she got used to the tape recorder which they took along. She made herself look upon it as a necessity rather than ostentation.

Eileen was dying for a cigarette.

'May I smoke, Arch?'

'We're amongst friends, aren't we?'

Eileen did not answer that. And Arch fetched the ash-tray they kept handy for those who needed it.

Nora in the kitchen dropped the beans. Everybody heard, but Arch asked Jum for a few tips on investments, as he always did when Nora happened to be out of the room. Nora had some idea that the Stock Exchange was immoral.

Then Nora brought the dish of little, pale tinned peas.

'Ah! *Pet—ty pwah!*' said Jum.

He formed his full, and rather greasy lips into a funnel through which the little rounded syllables poured most impressively.

Nora forgot her embarrassment. She envied Jum his courage

in foreign languages. Although there were her lessons in Italian, she would never have dared utter in public.

'Can you bear *crêpes Suzette*?' Nora had to apologize.

'Lovely, darling.' Eileen smiled.

She would have swallowed a tiger. But was, *au fond*, at her gloomiest.

What was the betting Nora would drop the *crêpes Suzette*? It was those long, trembly hands, on which the turquoise ring looked too small and innocent. The Mackenzies were still in the semi-precious bracket in the days when they became engaged.

'How's the old bird-watching?'

Jum had to force himself, but after all he had drunk their wine.

Arch Mackenzie sat deeper in his chair, almost completely at his ease.

'Got some new tapes,' he said. 'We'll play them later. Went up to Kurrajong on Sunday, and got the bell-birds. I'll play you the lyre-bird, too. That was Mount Wilson.'

'Didn't we heard the lyre-bird last time?' Eileen asked.

Arch said:

'Yes.'

Deliberately.

'But wouldn't you like to hear it again? It's something of a collector's piece.'

Nora said they'd be more comfortable drinking their coffee in the lounge.

Then Arch fetched the tape recorder. He set it up on the Queen Anne walnut piecrust. It certainly was an impressive machine.

'I'll play you the lyre-bird.'

'The *pièce de résistance*? Don't you think we should keep it?'

'He can never wait for the lyre-bird.'

Nora had grown almost complacent. She sat holding her

coffee, smiling faintly through the steam. The children she had never had with Arch were about to enter.

'Delicious coffee,' Eileen said.

She had finished her filter-tips. She had never felt drearier.

The tape machine had begun to snuffle. There was quite an unusual amount of crackle. Perhaps it was the bush. Yes, that was it. The bush!

'Well, it's really quite remarkable how you people have the patience,' Eileen Wheeler had to say.

'Ssh!'

Arch Mackenzie was frowning. He had sat forward in the period chair.

'This is where it comes in.'

His face was tragic in the shaded light.

'Get it?' he whispered.

His hand was helping. Or commanding.

'Quite remarkable,' Eileen repeated.

Jum was shocked to realize he had only two days left in which to take up the ICI rights for old Thingummy.

Nora sat looking at her empty cup. But lovingly.

Nora could have been beautiful, Eileen saw. And suddenly felt old, she who had stripped once or twice at amusing parties. Nora Mackenzie did not know about that.

Somewhere in the depths of the bush Nora was calling that it had just turned four o'clock, but she had forgotten to pack the thermos.

The machine snuffled.

Arch Mackenzie was listening. He was biting his moustache.

'There's another passage soon.' He frowned.

'Darling,' Nora whispered, 'after the lyre-bird you might slip into the kitchen and change the bulb. It went while I was making the coffee.'

Arch Mackenzie's frown deepened. Even Nora was letting him down.

But she did not see. She was so in love.

It might have been funny if it was not also pathetic. People were horribly pathetic, Eileen Wheeler decided, who had her intellectual moments. She was also feeling sick. It was Nora's *crêpes Suzette*, lying like blankets.

'You'll realize there are one or two rough passages,' Arch said, coming forward when the tape had ended. 'I might cut it.'

'It could do with a little trimming,' Eileen agreed. 'But perhaps it's more natural without.'

Am I a what's-this, a masochist, she asked.

'Don't forget the kitchen bulb,' Nora prompted.

Very gently. Very dreamy.

Her hair had strayed, in full dowdiness, down along her white cheek.

'I'll give you the bell-birds for while I'm gone.'

Jum's throat had begun to rattle. He sat up in time, though, and saved his cup in the same movement.

'I remember the bell-birds,' he said.

'Not these ones, you don't. These are new. These are the very latest. The best bell-birds.'

Arch had started the tape, and stalked out of the room, as if to let the bell-birds themselves prove his point.

'It is one of our loveliest recordings,' Nora promised.

They all listened or appeared to.

When Nora said:

'Oh, dear' – getting up – 'I do believe' – panting almost – 'the bell-bird tape' – trembling – 'is damaged.'

Certainly the crackle was more intense.

'Arch will be so terribly upset.'

She had switched off the horrifying machine. With surprising skill for one so helpless. For a moment it seemed to Eileen Wheeler that Nora Mackenzie was going to hide the offending tape somewhere in her bosom. But she thought better of it, and put it aside on one of those little superfluous tables.

'Perhaps it's the machine that's broken,' suggested Jum.

'Oh, no,' said Nora, 'it's the tape. I know. We'll have to give you something else.'

'I can't understand,' – Eileen grinned – 'how you ever got around, Nora, to being mechanical.'

'If you're determined,' Nora said.

Her head was lowered in concentration.

'If you want a thing enough.'

She was fixing a fresh tape.

'And we do love our birds. Our Sundays together in the bush.'

The machine had begun its snuffling and shuffling again. Nora Mackenzie raised her head, as if launched on an invocation.

Two or three notes of bird-song fell surprisingly pure and clear, out of the crackle, into the beige and string-coloured room.

'This is one,' Nora said, 'I don't think I've ever heard before.'

She smiled, however, and listened to identify.

'Willy-Wagtails,' Nora said.

Willy-Wagtails were suited to tape. The song tumbled and exulted.

'It must be something,' Nora said, 'that Arch made while I was with Mother. There were a couple of Sundays when he did a little field-work on his own.'

Nora might have given way to a gentle melancholy for all she had foregone if circumstances had not heightened the pitch. There was Arch standing in the doorway. Blood streaming.

'Blasted bulb collapsed in my hand!'

'Oh, darling! Oh *dear*!' Nora cried.

The Wheelers were both fascinated. There was the blood dripping on the beige wall-to-wall.

How the willy-wagtails chortled.

Nora Mackenzie literally staggered at her husband, to take upon herself, if possible, the whole ghastly business.

'Come along, Arch,' she moaned. 'We'll fix. In just a minute,' Nora panted.

And simply by closing the door, she succeeded in blotting the situation, all but the drops of blood that were left behind on the carpet.

'Poor old Arch! Bleeding like a pig!' Jum Wheeler said, and laughed.

Eileen added:

'We shall suffer the willy-wags alone.'

Perhaps it was better like that. You could relax. Eileen began to pull. Her step-ins had eaten into her.

The willy-wagtails were at it again.

'Am I going crackers?' asked Jum. 'Listening to those bloody birds!'

When somebody laughed. Out of the tape. The Wheelers sat. Still.

Three-quarters of the bottle! Snuffle crackle. *Arch Mackenzie, you're a fair trimmer!* Again that rather brassy laughter.

'Well, I'll be blowed!' said Jum Wheeler.

'But that's Miss Cullen,' Eileen said.

The Wheeler spirits soared as surely as plummets dragged the notes of the wagtail down.

But it's far too rocky, and far too late. Besides, it's willy-wagtails we're after. How Miss Cullen laughed. *Willy-wagtails by moonlight!* Arch was less intelligible, as if he had listened to too many birds, and caught the habit. Snuffle crackle went the machine . . . *the buttons are not made to undo* . . . Miss Cullen informed. *Oh, stop it. Arch!* ARCH! *You're* TEARING *me!*

So that the merciless machine took possession of the room. There in the crackle of twigs, the stench of ants, the two Wheelers sat. There was that long, thin Harry Edwards, Eileen remembered, with bony wrists, had got her down behind the barn. She had hated it at first. All mirth had been exorcized from Miss Cullen's recorded laughter. Grinding out. Grinding out. So much of life was recorded by now. Returning late from a country dance, the Wheelers had fallen down amongst the sticks and stones, and made what is called love, and risen in the grey hours, to find themselves numb and bulging.

If only the tape, if you knew the trick with the wretched switch.

Jum Wheeler decided not to look at his wife. Little guilty, pockets were turning themselves out in his mind. That woman at the Locomotive Hotel. Pockets and pockets of putrefying trash. Down along the creek, amongst the tussocks and the sheep pellets, the sun burning his boy's skin, he played his overture to sex. Alone.

This sort of thing's all very well, Miss Cullen decided. *It's time we turned practical. Are you sure we can find our way back to the car?*

Always trundling. Crackling. But there were the blessed wagtails again.

'Wonder if they forgot the machine?'

'Oh, God! Hasn't the tape bobbed up in Pymble?'

A single willy-wagtail sprinkled its grace-notes through the stuffy room.

'Everything's all right,' Nora announced. 'He's calmer now. I persuaded him to take a drop of brandy.'

'That should fix him,' Jum said.

But Nora was listening to the lone wagtail. She was standing in the bush. Listening. The notes of bird-song falling like mountain water, when they were not chiselled in moonlight.

'There is nothing purer,' Nora said, 'than the song of the wagtail. Excepting Schubert,' she added, 'some of Schubert.'

She was so shyly glad it had occurred to her.

But the Wheelers just sat.

And again Nora Mackenzie was standing alone amongst the inexorable moonlit gums. She thought perhaps she had always felt alone, even with Arch, while grateful even for her loneliness.

'Ah, there you are!' Nora said.

It was Arch. He stood holding out his bandaged wound. Rather rigid. He could have been up for court martial.

'I've missed the willy-wagtails,' Nora said, raising her face to him, exposing her distress, like a girl. 'Some day you'll have to play it to me. When you've the time. And we can concentrate.'

The Wheelers might not have existed.

As for the tape it had discovered silence.

Arch mumbled they'd all better have something to drink.

Jum agreed it was a good idea.

'Positively brilliant,' Eileen said.

V. S. NAIPAUL

V. S. NAIPAUL (1932–) Born in Trinidad, educated there and at Oxford. His first novel, The Mystic Masseur, *was published in 1957. Though much of his best fiction has been set in Trinidad (notably* A House for Mr Biswas, *1961), he has written travel books and history* (The Loss of El Dorado, *1969).* Miguel Street *(from which 'The Thing without a Name' comes) is a collection of linked short stories set in Port of Spain, Trinidad. It was the first book Naipaul wrote but was not published until after his first two novels.*

The Thing without a name

The only thing that Popo, who called himself a carpenter, ever built was the little galvanized-iron workshop under the mango tree at the back of his yard. And even that he didn't quite finish. He couldn't be bothered to nail on the sheets of galvanized-iron for the roof, and kept them weighted down with huge stones. Whenever there was a high wind the roof made a frightening banging noise and seemed ready to fly away.

And yet Popo was never idle. He was always busy hammering and sawing and planing. I liked watching him work. I liked the smell of the woods – cyp and cedar and crapaud. I liked the colour of the shavings, and I liked the way the saw-dust powdered Popo's kinky hair.

'What you making, Mr Popo?' I asked.

Popo would always say, 'Ha, boy! That's the question. I making the thing without a name.'

I liked Popo for that. I thought he was a poetic man.

One day I said to Popo, 'Give me something to make.'

'What you want to make?' he said.

It was hard to think of something I really wanted.

'You see,' Popo said. 'You thinking about the thing without a name.'

Eventually I decided on an egg-stand.

'Who you making it for?' Popo asked.

'Ma.'

He laughed. 'Think she going to use it?'

My mother was pleased with the egg-stand, and used it for about a week. Then she seemed to forget all about it; and began putting the eggs in bowls or plates, just as she did before.

And Popo laughed when I told him. He said, 'Boy, the only thing to make is the thing without a name.'

After I painted the tailoring sign for Bogart, Popo made me do one for him as well.

He took the little red stump of a pencil he had stuck over his ear and puzzled over the words. At first he wanted to announce himself as an architect; but I managed to dissuade him. He wasn't sure about the spelling. The finished sign said:

BUILDER AND CONTRACTOR
Carpenter
And Cabinet-Maker

And I signed my name, as sign-writer, in the bottom right-hand corner.

Popo liked standing up in front of the sign. But he had a little panic when people who didn't know about him came to inquire.

'The carpenter fellow?' Popo would say. 'He don't live here again.'

I thought Popo was a much nicer man than Bogart. Bogart said little to me; but Popo was always ready to talk. He talked about serious things, like life and death and work, and I felt he really liked talking to me.

Yet Popo was not a popular man in the street. They didn't think he was mad or stupid. Hat used to say, 'Popo too conceited, you hear.'

It was an unreasonable thing to say. Popo had the habit of taking a glass of rum to the pavement every morning. He never sipped the rum. But whenever he saw someone he knew he dipped his middle finger in the rum, licked it, and then waved to the man.

'We could buy rum too,' Hat used to say. 'But we don't show off like Popo.'

I myself never thought about it in that way, and one day I asked Popo about it.

Popo said, 'Boy, in the morning, when the sun shining and it still cool, and you just get up, it make you feel good to know that you could go out and stand up in the sun and have some rum.'

Popo never made any money. His wife used to go out and work, and this was easy, because they had no children. Popo said, 'Women and them like work. Man not make for work.'

Hat said, 'Popo is a man-woman. Not a proper man.'

Popo's wife had a job as a cook in a big house near my school. She used to wait for me in the afternoons and take me into the big kitchen and give me a lot of nice things to eat. The only thing I didn't like was the way she sat and watched me while I ate. It was as though I was eating for her. She asked me to call her Auntie.

She introduced me to the gardener of the big house. He was a good-looking brown man, and he loved his flowers. I liked the gardens he looked after. The flower-beds were always black and wet; and the grass green and damp and always cut. Sometimes he let me water the flower-beds. And he used to gather the cut grass into little bags which he gave me to take home to my mother. Grass was good for the hens.

One day I missed Popo's wife. She wasn't waiting for me.

Next morning I didn't see Popo dipping his finger in the glass of rum on the pavement.

And that evening I didn't see Popo's wife.

I found Popo sad in his workshop. He was sitting on a plank and twisting a bit of shaving around his fingers.

Popo said, 'Your auntie gone, boy.'

'Where, Mr Popo?'

'Ha, boy! That's the question,' and he pulled himself up there.

Popo found himself then a popular man. The news got around very quickly. And when Eddoes said one day, 'I wonder what happen to Popo. Like he got no more rum,' Hat jumped up and almost cuffed him. And then all the men began to gather in Popo's workshop, and they would talk about cricket and football and pictures – everything except women – just to try to cheer Popo up.

Popo's workshop no longer sounded with hammering and sawing. The sawdust no longer smelled fresh, and became black, almost like dirt. Popo began drinking a lot, and I didn't like him when he was drunk. He smelled of rum, and he used to cry and then grow angry and want to beat up everybody. That made him an accepted member of the gang.

Hat said, 'We was wrong about Popo. He is a man, like any of we.'

Popo liked the new companionship. He was at heart a loquacious man, and always wanted to be friendly with the men of the street and he was always surprised that he was not liked. So it looked as though he had got what he wanted. But Popo was not really happy. The friendship had come a little too late, and he found he didn't like it as much as he'd expected. Hat tried to get Popo interested in other women, but Popo wasn't interested.

Popo didn't think I was too young to be told anything.

'Boy, when you grow old as me,' he said once, 'you find that you don't care for the things you thought you woulda like if you coulda afford them.'

That was his way of talking, in riddles.

Then one day Popo left us.

Hat said, 'He don't have to tell me where he gone. He gone looking for he wife.'

Edward said, 'Think she going come back with he?'

Hat said, 'Let we wait and see.'

We didn't have to wait long. It came out in the papers. Hat said it was just what he expected. Popo had beaten up a man in Arima, the man had taken his wife away. It was the gardener who used to give me bags of grass.

Nothing much happened to Popo. He had to pay a fine, but

they let him off otherwise. The magistrates said that Popo had better not molest his wife again.

They made a calypso about Popo that was the rage that year. It was the road-march for the Carnival, and the Andrews Sisters sang it for an American recording company:

> *A certain carpenter feller went to Arima*
> *Looking for a mopsy called Emelda.*

It was a great thing for the street.

At school, I used to say, 'The carpenter feller was a good, good friend of mine.'

And, at cricket matches, and at the races, Hat used to say, 'Know him? God, I used to drink with that man night and day. Boy, he could carry his liquor.'

Popo wasn't the same man when he came back to us. He growled at me when I tried to talk to him, and he drove out Hat and the others when they brought a bottle of rum to the workshop.

Hat said, 'Woman send that man mad, you hear.'

But the old noises began to be heard once more from Popo's workshop. He was working hard, and I wondered whether he was still making the thing without a name. But I was too afraid to ask.

He ran an electric light to the workshop and began working in the night-time. Vans stopped outside his house and were always depositing and taking away things. Then Popo began painting his house. He used a bright green, and he painted the roof a bright red. Hat said, 'The man really mad.'

And added, 'Like he getting married again.'

Hat wasn't too far wrong. One day, about two weeks later, Popo returned, and he brought a woman with him. It was his wife. My auntie.

'You see the sort of thing woman is,' Hat commented. 'You see the sort of thing they like. Not the man. But the new house paint up, and all the new furniture inside it. I bet you if the man in Arima had a new house and new furnitures, she wouldnta come back with Popo.'

But I didn't mind. I was glad. It was good to see Popo standing outside with his glass of rum in the mornings and dipping his fingers into the rum and waving at his friends; and it was good to ask him again, 'What you making. Mr Popo?' and to get the old answer, 'Ha, boy! That's the question. I making the thing without a name.'

Popo returned very quickly to his old way of living, and he was still devoting his time to making the thing without a name. He had stopped working, and his wife got her job with the same people near my school.

People in the street were almost angry with Popo when his wife came back. They felt that all their sympathy had been mocked and wasted. And again Hat was saying, 'That blasted Popo too conceited, you hear.'

But this time Popo didn't mind.

He used to tell me, 'Boy, go home and pray tonight that you get happy like me.'

What happened afterwards happened so suddenly that we didn't even know it had happened. Even Hat didn't know about it until he read it in the papers. Hat always read the papers. He read them from about ten in the morning until about six in the evening.

Hat shouted out, 'But what is this I seeing?' and he showed us the headlines: CALYPSO CARPENTER JAILED.

It was a fantastic story. Popo had been stealing things left and right. All the new furnitures, as Hat called them, hadn't been made by Popo. He had stolen things and simply re-modelled them. He had stolen too much as a matter of fact, and had had to sell the things he didn't want. That was how he had been caught. And we understand now why the vans were always outside Popo's house. Even the paint and the brushes with which he had redecorated the house had been stolen.

Hat spoke for all of us when he said, 'That man too foolish. Why he had to sell what he thief? Just tell me that. Why?'

We agreed it was a stupid thing to do. But we felt deep inside ourselves that Popo was really a man, perhaps a bigger man than any of us.

And as for my auntie . . .

Hat said, 'How much jail he get? A year? With three months off for good behaviour, that's nine months in all. And I give she three months of good behaviour too. And after that, it ain't going to have no more Emelda in Miguel Street, you hear.'

But Emelda never left Miguel Street. She not only kept her job as cook, but she started taking in washing and ironing as well. No one in the street felt sorry that Popo had gone to jail because of the shame; after all that was a thing that could happen to any of us. They felt sorry only that Emelda was going to be left alone for so long.

He came back as a hero. He was one of the boys. He was a better man than either Hat or Bogart.

But for me, he had changed. And the change made me sad.

For Popo began working.

He began making morris chairs and tables and wardrobes for people.

And when I asked him, 'Mr Popo, when you going start making the thing without a name again?' he growled at me.

'You too troublesome,' he said. 'Go away quick, before I lay my hand on you.'

BERNARD MALAMUD

BERNARD MALAMUD (1914–) Born in Brooklyn, New York, and educated at the City College NY and Columbia. Has been a university teacher since 1939. His first novel The Natural *(1952) has a baseball theme. His fiction often involves Jewish themes (perhaps* The Fixer, *1966, filmed with Alan Bates, is the best-known example), and Jewish humour. But his writing is very varied. 'A Summer's Reading' comes from his first short story collection,* The Magic Barrel *(1958).*

A Summer's Reading

George Stoyonovich was a neighbourhood boy who had quit high school on an impulse when he was sixteen, run out of patience, and though he was ashamed every time he went looking for a job, when people asked him if he had finished and he had to say no, he never went back to school. This summer was a hard time for jobs and he had none. Having so much time on his hands, George thought of going to summer school, but the kids in his classes would be too young. He also considered registering in a night high school, only he didn't like the idea of the teachers always telling him what to do. He felt they had not respected him. The result was he stayed off the streets and in his room most of the day. He was close to twenty and had needs with the neighbourhood girls, but no money to spend, and he couldn't get more than an occasional few cents because his father was poor, and his sister Sophie, who resembled George, a tall bony girl of twenty-three, earned very little and what she had she kept for herself. Their mother was dead, and Sophie had to take care of the house.

Very early in the morning George's father got up to go to work in a fish market. Sophie left at about eight for her long ride in the subway to a cafeteria in the Bronx. George had his coffee by himself, then hung around in the house. When the house, a five-room railroad flat above a butcher store, got on his nerves he cleaned it up – mopped the floors with a wet mop and put things away. But most of the time he sat in his room. In the afternoons he listened to the ball game. Otherwise he had a couple of old copies of the *World Almanac* he had bought long ago, and he liked to read in them and also the magazines and newspapers that Sophie brought home, that had been left on the tables in the cafeteria. They were mostly picture magazines about movie stars and sports figures, also usually the *News* and *Mirror*. Sophie herself read whatever fell into her hands, although she sometimes read good books.

She once asked George what he did in his room all day and he said he read a lot too.

'Of what besides what I bring home? Do you ever read any worthwhile books?'

'Some,' George answered, although he really didn't. He had tried to read a book or two that Sophie had in the house but found he was in no mood for them. Lately he couldn't stand made-up stories, they got on his nerves. He wished he had some hobby to work at – as a kid he was good in carpentry, but where could he work at it? Sometimes during the day he went for walks, but mostly he did his walking after the hot sun had gone down and it was cooler in the streets.

In the evening after supper George left the house and wandered in the neighbourhood. During the sultry days some of the storekeepers and their wives sat in chairs on the thick, broken sidewalks in front of their shops, fanning themselves, and George walked past them and the guys hanging out on the candy store corner. A couple of them he had known his whole life, but nobody recognized each other. He had no place special to go, but generally, saving it till the last, he left the neighbourhood and walked for blocks till he came to a darkly lit little park with benches and trees and an iron railing, giving it a feeling of privacy. He sat on a bench here, watching the leafy trees and the flowers blooming on the inside of the railing, thinking of a better life for himself. He thought of the jobs he had had since he had quit school – delivery boy, stock clerk, runner, lately working in a factory – and he was dissatisfied with all of them. He felt he would some day like to have a job and live in a private house with a porch, on a street with trees. He wanted to have some dough in his pocket to buy things with, and a girl to go with, so as not to be lonely, especially on Saturday nights. He wanted people to like and respect him. He thought about these things often but mostly when he was alone at night. Around midnight he got up and drifted back to his hot and stony neighbourhood.

One time while on his walk George met Mr Cattanzara coming home very late from work. He wondered if he was drunk but then could tell he wasn't. Mr Cattanzara, a stocky, bald-headed man who worked in a change booth on an IRT station, lived on the next block after George's, above a shoe repair store. Nights, during the hot weather, he sat on his stoop in an undershirt, reading the *New York Times* in the light of the shoemaker's window. He read it from the first page to the last, then went up to sleep. And all the time he was reading the paper, his wife, a fat woman with a white face, leaned out of the window, gazing into the street, her thick white arms folded under her loose breast, on the window ledge.

Once in a while Mr Cattanzara came home drunk, but it was a quiet drunk. He never made any trouble, only walked stiffly up the street and slowly climbed the stairs into the hall. Though drunk, he looked the same as always, except for his tight walk, the quietness, and that his eyes were wet. George liked Mr Cattanzara because he remembered him giving him nickels to buy lemon ice with when he was a squirt. Mr Cattanzara was a different type than those in the neighbourhood. He asked different questions than the others when he met you, and he seemed to know what went on in all the newspapers. He read them, as his fat sick wife watched from the window.

'What are you doing with yourself this summer, George?' Mr Cattanzara asked. 'I see you walkin' around at nights.'

George felt embarrassed. 'I like to walk.'

'What are you doing' in the day now?'

'Nothing much right now. I'm waiting for a job.' Since it shamed him to admit he wasn't working, George said, 'I'm staying home – but I'm reading a lot to pick up my education.'

Mr Cattanzara looked interested. He mopped his hot face with a red handkerchief.

'What are you readin'?'

George hesitated, then said, 'I got a list of books in the library once, and now I'm gonna read them this summer.' He felt strange and a little unhappy saying this, but he wanted Mr Cattanzara to respect him.

'How many books are there on it?'

'I never counted them. Maybe around a hundred.'

Mr Cattanzara whistled through his teeth.

'I figure if I did that,' George went on earnestly, 'it would help me in my education. I don't mean the kind they give you in high school. I want to know different things than they learn there, if you know what I mean.'

The change maker nodded. 'Still and all, one hundred books is a pretty big load for one summer.'

'It might take longer.'

'After you're finished with some, maybe you and I can shoot the breeze about them?' said Mr Cattanzara.

'When I'm finished,' George answered.

Mr Cattanzara went home and George continued on his walk. After that, though he had the urge to, George did nothing different from usual. He still took his walks at night, ending up in the little park. But one evening the shoemaker on the next block stopped George to say he was a good boy, and George figured that Mr Cattanzara had told him all about the books he was reading. From the shoemaker it must have gone down the street, because George saw a couple of people smiling kindly at him, though nobody spoke to him personally. He felt a little better around the neighbourhood and liked it more, though not so much he would want to live in it for ever. He had never exactly disliked the people in it, yet he had never liked them much either. It was the fault of the neighbourhood.

To his surprise, George found out that his father and Sophie knew about his reading too. His father was too shy to say anything about it – he was never much of a talker in his whole life – but Sophie was softer to George, and she showed him in other ways she was proud of him.

As the summer went on George felt in a good mood about things. He cleaned the house every day, as a favour to Sophie, and he enjoyed the ball games more. Sophie gave him a buck a week allowance, and though it still wasn't enough and he had to use it carefully, it was a helluva lot better than just having two bits now and then. What he bought with the money – cigarettes mostly, an occasional beer or movie ticket – he got a big kick out of. Life wasn't so bad if you knew how to appreciate it. Occasionally he bought a paperback book from the news-stand, but he never got around to reading it, though he was glad to have a couple of books in his room. But he read thoroughly Sophie's magazines and newspapers. And at night was the most enjoyable time, because when he passed the storekeepers sitting outside their stores, he could tell they regarded him highly. He walked erect, and though he did not say much to them, or they to him, he could feel approval on all sides. A couple of nights he felt so good that he skipped the park at the end of the evening. He just wandered in the neighbourhood, where people had known him from the time he was a kid playing punchball whenever there was a game of it going; he wandered there, then came home and got undressed for bed, feeling fine.

For a few weeks he had talked only once with Mr Cattanzara, and though the change maker had said nothing more about the books, asked no questions, his silence made George a little uneasy. For a while George didn't pass in front of Mr Cattanzara's house any more, until one night, forgetting himself, he approached it from a different direction than he usually did when he did. It was already past midnight. The street, except for one or two people, was deserted, and George was surprised when he saw Mr Cattanzara still reading his newspaper by the light of the street lamp overhead. His impulse was to stop at the stoop and talk to him. He wasn't sure what he wanted to say, though he felt the words would come when he began to talk; but the more he thought about it, the more the idea scared him, and he decided he'd better not. He even considered beating it home by another street, but he was too near Mr Cattanzara, and the change maker might see him as he ran, and get annoyed. So George unobtrusively crossed the street, trying to make it seem as if he had to look in a store window on the other side, which he did, and then went on, uncomfortable at what he was doing. He feared Mr Cattanzara would glance up from his paper and call him a dirty rat for walking on the other side of the street, but all he did was sit there, sweating through his undershirt, his bald head shining in the dim light as he read his *Times*, and upstairs his fat wife leaned out of the window, seeming to read the paper along with him. George thought she would spy him and yell out to Mr Cattanzara, but she never moved her eyes off her husband.

George made up his mind to stay away from the change maker until he had got some of his softback books read, but when he started them and saw they were mostly story books, he lost interest and didn't bother to finish them. He lost his interest in reading other things too. Sophie's magazines and newspapers went unread. She saw them piling up on a chair in his room and asked why he was no longer looking at them, and George told her it was because of all the other reading he had to do. Sophie said she had guessed that was it. So for most of the day, George had the radio on, turning to music when he was sick of the human voice. He kept the house fairly neat, and Sophie said nothing on the days when he neglected it. She was still kind and gave him his extra buck, though things weren't so good for him as they had been before.

But they were good enough, considering. Also his night

walks invariably picked him up, no matter how bad the day was. Then one night George saw Mr Cattanzara coming down the street towards him. George was about to turn and run but he recognized from Mr Cattanzara's walk that he was drunk, and if so, probably he would not even bother to notice him. So George kept on walking straight ahead until he came abreast of Mr Cattanzara and though he felt wound up enough to pop into the sky, he was not surprised when Mr Cattanzara passed him without a word, walking slowly, his face and body stiff. George drew a breath in relief at his narrow escape, when he heard his name called, and there stood Mr Cattanzara at his elbow, smelling like the inside of a beer barrel. His eyes were sad as he gazed at George, and George felt so intensely uncomfortable he was tempted to shove the drunk aside and continue on his walk.

But he couldn't act that way to him, and, besides, Mr Cattanzara took a nickel out of his pants pocket and handed it to him.

'Go buy yourself a lemon ice, Georgie.'

'It's not that time any more, Mr Cattanzara,' George said, 'I am a big guy now.'

'No, you ain't,' said Mr Cattanzara, to which George made no reply he could think of.

'How are all your books comin' along now?' Mr Cattanzara asked. Though he tried to stand steady, he swayed a little.

'Fine, I guess,' said George, feeling the red crawling up his face.

'You ain't sure?' The change maker smiled slyly, a way George had never seen him smile.

'Sure I'm sure. They're fine.'

Though his head swayed in little arcs, Mr Cattanzara's eyes were steady. He had small blue eyes which could hurt if you looked at them too long.

'George,' he said, 'name me one book on that list that you read this summer, and I will drink to your health.'

'I don't want anybody drinking to me.'

'Name me one so I can ask you a question on it. Who can tell, if it's a good book maybe I might wanna read it myself.'

George knew he looked passable on the outside, but inside he was crumbling apart.

Unable to reply, he shut his eyes, but when – years later – he opened them, he saw that Mr Cattanzara had, out of pity, gone away, but in his ears he still heard the words he had said when he left: 'George, don't do what I did.'

The next night he was afraid to leave his room, and though Sophie argued with him he wouldn't open the door.

'What are you doing in there?' she asked.

'Nothing.'

'Are you reading?'

'No.'

She was silent a minute, then asked, 'Where do you keep the books you read? I never see any in your room outside of a few cheap trashy ones.'

He wouldn't tell her.

'In that case you're not worth a buck of my hard-earned money. Why should I break my back for you? Go on out, you bum, and get a job.'

He stayed in his room for almost a week, except to sneak into the kitchen when nobody was home. Sophie railed at him, then begged him to come out, and his old father wept, but George wouldn't budge, though the weather was terrible and his small room stifling. He found it very hard to breathe, each breath was like drawing a flame into his lungs.

One night, unable to stand the heat any more, he burst into the street at one a.m., a shadow of himself. He hoped to sneak to the park without being seen, but there were people all over the block, wilted and listless, waiting for a breeze. George lowered his eyes and walked, in disgrace, away from them, but before long he discovered they were still friendly to him. He figured Mr Cattanzara hadn't told on him. Maybe when he woke up out of his drunk the next morning, he had forgotten all about meeting George. George felt his confidence slowly come back to him.

That same night a man on a street corner asked him if it was true that he had finished reading so many books, and George admitted he had. The man said it was a wonderful thing for a boy his age to read so much.

'Yeah,' George said, but he felt relieved. He hoped nobody would mention the books any more, and when, after a couple of days, he accidentally met Mr Cattanzara again, *he* didn't, though George had the idea he was the one who had started the rumour that he had finished all the books.

One evening in the fall, George ran out of his house to the library, where he hadn't been in years. There were books all over the place, wherever he looked, and though he was struggling to control an inward trembling, he easily counted off a hundred, then sat down at a table to read.

JOHN CHEEVER

JOHN CHEEVER (1912–) Born in Quincy, Massachusetts, USA. Novelist and short story writer. Best known for his hilarious novel The Wapshot Chronicle (1957) *and its sequel* The Wapshot Scandal. *Many of his short stories first appeared in* The New Yorker, *the weekly periodical that nurtured almost a school of humorists, and influenced many other American satirical writers. 'The Swimmer', subsequently filmed with Burt Lancaster, first appeared in book form in* The Brigadier and the Golf Widow (1964). *It clearly pays homage to Scott Fitzgerald and can be read as a parable of the 'Jazz Age'.*

The Swimmer

It was one of those midsummer Sundays when everyone sits around saying: 'I *drank* too much last night.' You might have heard it whispered by the parishioners leaving church, heard it from the lips of the priest himself, struggling with his cassock in the *vestiarium*, heard it from the golf links and the tennis courts, heard it from the wild-life preserve where the leader of the Audubon group was suffering from a terrible hang-over. 'I *drank* too much,' said Donald Westerhazy. 'We all *drank* too much,' said Lucinda Merrill. 'It must have been the wine,' said Helen Westerhazy. 'I *drank* too much of that claret.'

This was at the edge of the Westerhazys' pool. The pool, fed by an artesian well with a high iron content, was a pale shade of green. It was a fine day. In the west there was a massive stand of cumulus cloud so like a city seen from a distance – from the bow of an approaching ship – that it might have had a name. Lisbon. Hackensack. The sun was hot. Neddy Merrill sat by the green water, one hand in it, one around a glass of gin. He was a slender man – he seemed to have the especial slenderness of youth – and while he was far from young he had slid down his banister that morning and given the bronze backside of Aphrodite on the hall table a smack, as he jogged toward the smell of coffee in his dining-room. He might have been compared to a summer's day, particularly the last hours of one, and while he lacked a tennis racket or a sail bag the impression was definitely one of youth, sport and clement weather. He had been swimming and now he was breathing deeply, stertorously as if he could gulp into his lungs the components of that moment, the heat of the sun, the intenseness of his pleasure. It all seemed to flow into his chest. His own house stood in Bullet Park, eight miles to the south, where his four beautiful daughters would have had their lunch and might be playing tennis. Then it occurred to him that by taking a dogleg to the southwest he could reach his home by water.

His life was not confining and the delight he took in this observation could not be explained by its suggestion of escape. He seemed to see, with a cartographer's eye, that string of swimming pools, that quasi-subterranean stream that curved across the county. He had made a discovery, a contribution to modern geography; he would name the stream Lucinda after his wife. He was not a practical joker nor was he a fool but he was determinedly original and had a vague and modest idea of himself as a legendary figure. The day was beautiful and it seemed to him that a long swim might enlarge and celebrate its beauty.

He took off a sweater that was hung over his shoulders and dived in. He had an inexplicable contempt for men who did not hurl themselves into pools. He swam a choppy crawl, breathing either every stroke or every fourth stroke and counting somewhere well in the back of his mind the one-two one-two of a flutter kick. It was not a serviceable stroke for long distances but the domestication of swimming had saddled the sport with some customs and in his part of the world a crawl was customary. To be embraced and sustained by the light green water was less a pleasure, it seemed, than the resumption of a natural condition, and he would have liked to swim without trunks, but this was not possible, considering his project. He hoisted himself up on to the far curb – he never used the ladder – and started across the lawn. When Lucinda asked where he was going he said he was going to swim home.

The only maps and charts he had to go by were remembered or imaginary but these were clear enough. First there were the Grahams, the Hammers, the Lears, the Howlands, and the

Crosscups. He would cross Ditmar Street to the Bunkers and come, after a short portage, to the Levys, the Welchers, and the public pool in Lancaster. Then there were the Hallorans, the Sachses, the Biswangers, Shirley Adams, the Gilmartins, and the Clydes. The day was lovely, and that he lived in a world so generously supplied with water seemed like a clemency, a beneficence. His heart was high and he ran across the grass. Making his way home by an uncommon route gave him the feeling that he was a pilgrim, an explorer, a man with a destiny, and he knew that he would find friends all along the way; friends would line the banks of the Lucinda River.

He went through a hedge that separated the Westerhazys' land from the Grahams', walked under some flowering apple trees, passed the shed that housed their pump and filter, and came out at the Grahams' pool. 'Why, Neddy,' Mrs Graham said, 'what a marvellous surprise. I've been trying to get you on the phone all morning. Here, let me get you a drink.' He saw then, like any explorer, that the hospitable customs and traditions of the natives would have to be handled with diplomacy if he was ever going to reach his destination. He did not want to mystify or seem rude to the Grahams nor did he have the time to linger there. He swam the length of their pool and joined them in the sun and was rescued, a few minutes later, by the arrival of two carloads of friends from Connecticut. During the uproarious reunions he was able to slip away. He went down by the front of the Grahams' house, stepped over a thorny hedge, and crossed a vacant lot to the Hammers'. Mrs Hammer, looking up from her roses, saw him swim by although she wasn't quite sure who it was. The Lears heard him splashing past the open windows of their living-room. The Howlands and the Crosscups were away. After leaving the Howlands' he crossed Ditmar Street and started for the Bunkers' where he could hear, even at that distance, the noise of a party.

The water refracted the sound of voice and laughter and seemed to suspend it in mid-air. The Bunkers' pool was on a rise and he climbed some stairs to a terrace where twenty-five or thirty men and women were drinking. The only person in the water was Rusty Towers, who floated there on a rubber raft. Oh how bonny and lush were the banks of the Lucinda River! Prosperous men and women gathered by the sapphire-coloured waters while caterer's men in white coats passed them cold gin. Overhead a red de Haviland trainer was circling around and around and around in the sky with something like the glee of a child in a swing. Ned felt a passing affection for the scene, a tenderness for the gathering, as if it was something he might touch. In the distance he heard thunder. As soon as Enid Bunker saw him she began to scream: 'Oh look who's here! What a marvellous surprise! When Lucinda said that you couldn't come I thought I'd *die.*' She made her way to him through the crowd, and when they had finished kissing she led him to the bar, a progress that was slowed by the fact that he stopped to kiss eight or ten other women and shake the hands of as many men. A smiling bartender he had seen at a hundred parties gave him a gin and tonic and he stood by the bar for a moment, anxious not to get stuck in any conversation that would delay his voyage. When he seemed about to be surrounded he dived in and swam close to the side to avoid colliding with Rusty's raft. At the far end of the pool he bypassed the Tomlinsons with a broad smile and jogged up the garden path. The gravel cut his feet but this was the only unpleasantness. The party was confined to the pool, and as he went toward the house he heard the brilliant watery sound of voices fade, heard the noise of a radio from the Bunkers' kitchen, where someone was listening to a ball game. Sunday afternoon. He made his way through the parked cars and down the grassy border of their driveway to Alewives' Lane. He did not want to be seen on the road in his bathing trunks but there was no traffic and he made the short distance to the Levys' driveway, marked with a private property sign and a green tube for the *New York Times*. All the doors and windows of the big house were open but there were no signs of life; not even a dog barked. He went around the side of the house to the pool and saw that the Levys had only recently left. Glasses and bottles and dishes of nuts were on a table at the deep end, where there was a bathhouse or gazebo, hung with Japanese lanterns. After swimming the pool he got himself a glass and poured a drink. It was his fourth or fifth drink and he had swum nearly half the length of the Lucinda River. He felt tired, clean, and pleased at that moment to be alone; pleased with everything.

It would storm. The stand of cumulus cloud – that city – had risen and darkened, and while he sat there he heard the percussiveness of thunder again. The de Haviland trainer was still circling overhead and it seemed to Ned that he could almost hear the pilot laugh with pleasure in the afternoon; but when there was another peal of thunder he took off for home. A train whistle blew and he wondered what time it had gotten to be. Four? Five? He thought of the provincial station at that hour, where a waiter, his tuxedo concealed by a raincoat, a dwarf with some flowers wrapped in newspaper, and a woman who had been crying would be waiting for the local. It was suddenly growing dark; it was that moment when the pin-headed birds seem to organize their song into some acute and knowledgeable recognition of the storm's approach. Then there was a fine noise of rushing water from the crown of an oak at his back, as if a spigot there had been turned. Then the noise of fountains came from the crowns of all the tall trees. Why did he love storms, what was the meaning of his excitement when the door sprang open and the rain wind fled rudely up the stairs, why had the simple task of shutting the windows of an old house seemed fitting and urgent, why did the first watery notes of a storm wind have for him the unmistakable sound of good news, cheer, glad tidings? Then there was an explosion, a smell of cordite, and rain lashed the Japanese lanterns that Mrs Levy had bought in Kyoto the year before last, or was it the year before that?

He stayed in the Levys' gazebo until the storm had passed. The rain had cooled the air and he shivered. The force of the wind had stripped a maple of its red and yellow leaves and scattered them over the grass and the water. Since it was midsummer the tree must be blighted, and yet he felt a peculiar sadness at this sign of autumn. He braced his shoulders, emptied his glass, and started for the Welchers' pool. This meant crossing the Lindleys' riding ring and he was surprised to find it overgrown with grass and all the jumps dismantled. He wondered if the Lindleys had sold their horses or gone away for the summer and put them out to board. He seemed to remember having heard something about the Lindleys and their horses but the memory was unclear. On he went, barefoot through the wet grass, to the Welchers', where he found their pool was dry.

This breach in his chain of water disappointed him absurdly, and he felt like some explorer who seeks a torrential headwater and finds a dead stream. He was disappointed and mystified. It was common enough to go away for the summer but no one ever drained his pool. The Welchers had definitely gone away. The pool furniture was folded, stacked, and covered with a tarpaulin. The bathhouse was locked. All the windows of the house were shut, and when he went around to the driveway in front he saw a for-sale sign nailed to a tree. When had he last heard from the Welchers – when, that is, had he and Lucinda last regretted an invitation to dine with them? It seemed only a week or so ago. Was his memory failing or had he so disciplined it in the repression of unpleasant facts that he had damaged his sense of the truth? Then in the distance he heard the sound of a tennis game. This cheered him, cleared away all his apprehensions and let him regard the overcast sky and the cold air with indifference. This was the day that Neddy Merrill

swam across the county. That was the day! He started off then
for his most difficult portage.

Had you gone for a Sunday afternoon ride that day you
might have seen him, close to naked, standing on the shoulders
of route 424, waiting for a chance to cross. You might have
wondered if he was the victim of foul play, had his car broken
down, or was he merely a fool. Standing barefoot in the depo-
sits of he highway – beer cans, rags, and blowout patches –
exposed to all kinds of ridicule, he seemed pitiful. He had
known when he started that this was a part of his journey – it
had been on his maps – but confronted with the lines of traffic,
worming through the summery light, he found himself unprepared. He was laughed at, jeered at, a beer can was thrown at
him, and he had no dignity or humour to bring to the situation. He could have gone back, back to the Westerhazys',
where Lucinda would still be sitting in the sun. He had signed
nothing, vowed nothing, pledged nothing not even to himself.
Why, believing as he did, that all human obduracy was sus-
ceptible to common sense, was he unable to turn back? Why
was he determined to complete his journey even if it meant
putting his life in danger? At what point had this prank, this
joke, this piece of horseplay become serious? He could not go
back, he could not even recall with any clearness the green
water at the Westerhazys', the sense of inhaling the day's components, the friendly and relaxed voices saying that they had
drunk too much. In the space of an hour, more or less, he had
covered a distance that made his return impossible.

An old man, tooling down the highway at fifteen miles an
hour, let him get to the middle of the road, where there was a
grass divider. Here he was exposed to the ridicule of the north-
bound traffic, but after ten or fifteen minutes he was able to
cross. From here he had only a short walk to the Recreation
Centre at the edge of the Village of Lancaster, where there
were some handball courts and a public pool.

The effect of the water on voices, the illusion of brilliance and suspense, was the same here as it had been at the Bunkers' but the sounds here were louder, harsher, and more shrill, and as soon as he entered the crowded enclosure he was confronted with regimentation. 'ALL SWIMMERS MUST TAKE A SHOWER BEFORE USING THE POOL. ALL SWIMMERS MUST USE THE FOOT-BATH. ALL SWIMMERS MUST WEAR THEIR IDENTIFICATION DISCS.' He took a shower, washed his feet in a cloudy and bitter solution and made his way to the edge of the water. It stank of chlorine and looked to him like a sink. A pair of lifeguards in a pair of towers blew police whistles at what seemed to be regular intervals and abused the swimmers through the public address system. Neddy remembered the sapphire water at the Bunkers with longing and thought that he might contaminate himself – damage his own prosperousness and charm – by swimming in this murk, but he reminded himself that he was an explorer, a pilgrim, and that this was merely a stagnant bend in the Lucinda River. He dived, scowling with distaste, into the chlorine and had to swim with his head above water to avoid collisions, but even so he was bumped into, splashed and jostled. When he got to the shallow end both lifeguards were shouting at him: 'Hey, you, you without the identification disc, get outa the water.' He did, but they had no way of pursuing him and he went through the reek of suntan oil and chlorine out through the hurricane fence and passed the handball courts. By crossing the road he entered the wooded part of the Halloran estate. The woods were not cleared and the footing was treacherous and difficult until he reached the lawn and the clipped beech hedge that encircled their pool.

The Hallorans were friends, an elderly couple of enormous wealth who seemed to bask in the suspicion that they might be Communists. They were zealous reformers but they were not Communists, and yet when they were accused, as they some-times were, of subversion, it seemed to gratify and excite them. Their beech hedge was yellow and he guessed this had been blighted like the Levys' maple. He called hullo, hullo, to warn the Hallorans of his approach, to palliate his invasion of their privacy. The Hallorans, for reasons that had never been explained to him, did not wear bathing suits. No explanations were in order, really. Their nakedness was a detail in their uncompromising zeal for reform and he stepped politely out of his trunks before he went through the opening in the hedge.

Mrs Halloran, a stout woman with white hair and a serene face, was reading the *Times*. Mr Halloran was taking beech leaves out of the water with a scoop. They seemed not surprised or displeased to see him. Their pool was perhaps the oldest in the county, a fieldstone rectangle, fed by a brook. It had no filter or pump and its waters were the opaque gold of the stream.

'I'm swimming across the county,' Ned said.

'Why, I didn't know one could,' exclaimed Mrs Halloran.

'Well. I've made it from the Westerhazys',' Ned said. 'That must be about four miles.'

He left his trunks at the deep end, walked to the shallow end, and swam this stretch. As he was pulling himself out of the water he heard Mrs Halloran say: 'We've been *terribly* sorry to hear about all your misfortunes, Neddy.'

'My misfortunes?' Ned asked. 'I don't know what you mean.'

'Why, we heard that you'd sold the house and that your poor children ...'

'I don't recall having sold the house,' Ned said, 'and the girls are at home.'

'Yes,' Mrs Halloran sighed. 'Yes ...' Her voice filled the air with an unreasonable melancholy and Ned spoke briskly. 'Thank you for the swim.'

'Well, have a nice trip,' said Mrs Halloran.

Beyond the hedge he pulled on his trunks and fastened them. They were loose and he wondered if, during the space of an

74

afternoon, he could have lost some weight. He was cold and he was tired and the naked Hallorans and their dark water had depressed him. The swim was too much for his strength but how could he have guessed this, sliding down the banister that morning and sitting in the Westerhazys' sun? His arms were lame. His legs felt rubbery and ached at the joints. The worst of it was the cold in his bones and the feeling that he might never be warm again. Leaves were falling down around him and he smelled woodsmoke on the wind. Who would be burning wood at this time of year?

He needed a drink. Whiskey would warm him, pick him up, carry him through the last of his journey, refresh his feeling that it was original and valorous to swim across the county. Channel swimmers took brandy. He needed a stimulant. He crossed the lawn in front of the Hallorans' house and went down a little path to where they had built a house for their only daughter Helen and her husband Eric Sachs. The Sachses' pool was small and he found Helen and her husband there.

'Oh, *Neddy*,' Helen said. 'Did you lunch at Mother's?'

'Not *really*,' Ned said. 'I did stop to see your parents.' This seemed to be explanation enough. 'I'm terribly sorry to break in on you like this but I've taken a chill and I wonder if you'd give me a drink.'

'Why, I'd *love* to,' Helen said, 'but there hasn't been anything in this house to drink since Eric's operation. That was three years ago.'

Was he losing his memory, had his gift for concealing painful facts let him forget that he had sold his house, that his children were in trouble, and that his friend had been ill? His eyes slipped from Eric's face to his abdomen, where he saw three pale, sutured scars, two of them at least a foot long. Gone was his navel, and what, Neddy thought, would the roving hand, bed-checking one's gifts at 3 a.m., make of a belly with no navel, no link to birth, this breach in the succession?

'I'm sure you can get a drink at the Biswangers',' Helen

said. 'They're having an enormous do. You can hear it from here. Listen!'

She raised her head and from across the road, the lawns, the gardens, the woods, the fields, he heard again the brilliant noise of voices over water. 'Well, I'll get wet,' he said, still feeling that he had no freedom of choice about his means of travel. He dived into the Sachses' cold water and, gasping, close to drowning, made his way from one end of the pool to the other. 'Lucinda and I want *terribly* to see you,' he said over his shoulder, his face set toward the Biswangers'. 'We're sorry it's been so long and we'll call you *very* soon.'

He crossed some fields to the Biswangers' and the sounds of revelry there. They would be honoured to give him a drink, they would be happy to give him a drink, they would in fact be lucky to give him a drink. The Biswangers invited him and Lucinda for dinner four times a year, six weeks in advance. They were always rebuffed and yet they continued to send out their invitations, unwilling to comprehend the rigid and undemocratic realities of their society. They were the sort of people who discussed the price of things at cocktails, exchanged market tips during dinner, and after dinner told dirty stories to mixed company. They did not belong to Neddy's set – they were not even on Lucinda's Christmas card list. He went toward their pool with feelings of indifference, charity, and some unease, since it seemed to be getting dark and these were the longest days of the year. The party when he joined it was noisy and large. Grace Biswanger was the kind of hostess who asked the optometrist, the veterinarian, the real-estate dealer and the dentist. No one was swimming and the twilight, reflected on the water of the pool, had a wintry gleam. There was a bar and he started for this. When Grace Biswanger saw him she came toward him, not affectionately as he had every right to expect, but bellicosely.

'Why, this party has everything,' she said loudly, 'including a gate crasher.'

She could not deal him a social blow – there was no question about this and he did not flinch. 'As a gate crasher,' he asked politely, 'do I rate a drink?'

'Suit yourself,' she said. 'You don't seem to pay much attention to invitations.'

She turned her back on him and joined some guests, and he went to the bar and ordered a whiskey. The bartender served him but he served him rudely. His was a world in which the caterer's men kept the social score, and to be rebuffed by a part-time barkeep meant that he had suffered some loss of social esteem. Or perhaps the man was new and uninformed. Then he heard Grace at his back say: 'They went for broke overnight – nothing but income – and he showed up drunk one Sunday and asked us to loan him five thousand dollars. . . .' She was always talking about money. It was worse than eating your peas off a knife. He dived into the pool, swam its length and went away.

The next pool on his list, the last but two, belonged to his old mistress, Shirley Adams. If he had suffered any injuries at the Biswangers' they would be cured here. Love – sexual roughhouse in fact – was the supreme elixir, the painkiller, the brightly coloured pill that would put the spring back into his step, the joy of life in his heart. They had had an affair last week, last month, last year. He couldn't remember. It was he who had broken it off, his was the upper hand, and he stepped through the gate of the wall that surrounded her pool with nothing so considered as self-confidence. It seemed in a way to be his pool as the lover, particularly the illicit lover, enjoys the possessions of his mistress with an authority unknown to holy matrimony. She was there, her hair the colour of brass, but her figure, at the edge of the lighted, cerulean water, excited in him no profound memories. It had been, he thought, a light-hearted affair, although she had wept when he broke it off. She seemed confused to see him and he wondered if she was still wounded. Would she, God forbid, weep again?

'What do you want?' she asked.

'I'm swimming across the county.'

'Good Christ. Will you ever grow up?'

'What's the matter?'

'If you've come here for money,' she said, 'I won't give you another cent.'

'You could give me a drink.'

'I could but I won't. I'm not alone.'

'Well, I'm on my way.'

He dived in and swam the pool, but when he tried to haul himself up on to the curb he found that the strength in his arms and his shoulders had gone, and he paddled to the ladder and climbed out. Looking over his shoulder he saw, in the lighted bathhouse, a young man. Going out onto the dark lawn he smelled chrysanthemums or marigolds – some stubborn autumnal fragrance – on the night air, strong as gas. Looking overhead he saw that the stars had come out, but why should he seem to see Andromeda, Cepheus, and Cassiopeia? What had become of the constellations of midsummer? He began to cry.

It was probably the first time in his adult life that he had ever felt so miserable, cold, tired, and bewildered. He could not understand the rudeness of the caterer's barkeep or the rudeness of a mistress who had come to him on her knees and showered his trousers with tears. He had swum too long, he had been immersed too long, and his nose and his throat were sore from the water. What he needed then was a drink, some company, and some clean dry clothes, and while he could have cut directly across the road to his home he went on to the Gilmartins' pool. Here, for the first time in his life, he did not dive but went down the steps into the icy water and swam a hobble side-stroke that he might have learned as a youth. He staggered with fatigue on his way to the Clydes' and paddled the length of the pool, stopping again and again with his hand on the curb to rest. He climbed the ladder and wondered if he had the strength to get home. He had done what he wanted, he had swum the county, but he was so stupefied with exhaustion that his triumph seemed vague. Stooped, holding on to the gateposts for support, he turned up the driveway of his own house.

The place was dark. Was it so late that they had all gone to bed? Had Lucinda stayed at the Westerhazys' for supper? Had the girls joined her there or gone someplace else? Hadn't they agreed, as they usually did on Sunday, to regret all their invitations and stay at home? He tried the garage doors to see what cars were in but the doors were locked and rust came off the handles onto his hands. Going toward the house, he saw that the force of the thunderstorm had knocked one of the rain gutters loose. It hung down over the front door like an umbrella rib, but it could be fixed in the morning. The house was locked, and he thought that the stupid cook or the stupid maid must have locked the place up until he remembered that it had been some time since they had employed a maid or a cook. He shouted, pounded on the door, tried to force it with his shoulder, and then, looking in at the windows, saw that the place was empty.

EDMUND WILSON

EDMUND WILSON (1895–1972) Born in Red Bank, New Jersey, USA. Educated at Princeton. Playwright, poet, novelist (I Thought of Daisy, *1929*), *short story writer* (Memoirs of Hecate County, *1946, revised 1960*), *which includes* 'The Man Who Shot Snapping Turtles'. *Critic of massive influence* (Axel's Castle, *1931*, The Shock of Recognition, *1943*). *Never an academic, his mind ranged widely: travel, anthropology, history, politics have all engaged his attention. His learning was extraordinary; for example in order to write* The Scrolls from the Dead Sea (*1955*) *he taught himself Hebrew. He married Mary McCarthy, the American novelist.*

The Man Who Shot Snapping Turtles

In the days when I lived in Hecate County, I had an uncomfortable neighbour, a man named Asa M. Stryker. He had at one time, he told me, taught chemistry in some sooty-sounding college in Pennsylvania, but he now lived on a little money which he had been 'lucky enough to inherit'! I had the feeling about him that somewhere in the background was defeat or frustration or disgrace. He was a bachelor and kept house with two servants – a cook and a man around the place. I never knew anyone to visit him, though he would occasionally go away for short periods – when, he would tell me, he was visiting his relatives.

Mr Stryker had a small pond on his place, and from the very first time I met him, his chief topic of conversation was the wild ducks that used to come to this pond. In his insensitive-sounding way he admired them, minutely observing their markings, and he cherished and protected them like pets. Several pairs, in fact, which he fed all the year round, settled permanently on the pond. He would call my attention in his hard accent to the richness of their chestnut browns; the ruddiness of their backs or breasts; their sharp contrasts of light with dark, and their white neck-rings and purple wing-bars, like the decorative liveries and insignia of some exalted order; the cupreous greens and blues that gave them the look of being expensively dressed.

Mr Stryker was particularly struck by the idea that there was something princely about them – something which, as he used to say, Frick or Charlie Schwab couldn't buy; and he would point out to me their majesty as they swam, cocking their heads with such dignity and nonchalantly wagging their tails. He was much troubled by the depredations of snapping turtles, which made terrible ravages on the ducklings. He would sit on his porch, he said, and see the little ducks disappear, as the turtles grabbed their feet and dragged them under, and feel sore at his helplessness to prevent it.

As he lost brood after brood in this way, the subject came, in fact, to obsess him. He had apparently hoped that his pond might be made a sort of paradise for ducks, in which they could breed without danger: he never shot them even in season and did not approve of their being shot at all. But sometimes not one survived the age when it was little enough to fall victim to the turtles.

These turtles he fought in a curious fashion. He would stand on the bank with a rifle and pot them when they stuck up their heads, sometimes hitting a duck by mistake. Only the ducks that were thus killed accidentally did he think it right to eat. One night when he had invited me to dine with him on one of them, I asked him why he did not protect the ducklings by shutting them up in a wire pen and providing them with a small pool to swim in. He told me that he had already decided to try this, and the next time I saw him he reported that the ducklings were doing finely.

Yet the pen, as it turned out later, did not permanently solve the problem, for the wild ducks, when they got old enough, flew out of it, and they were still young enough to be caught by the turtles. Mr Stryker could not, as he said, keep them captive all their lives. The thing was rather, he finally concluded, to try to get rid of the turtles, against which he was coming, I noted, to display a slightly morbid animosity, and, after a good deal of serious thought, he fixed upon an heroic method.

He had just come into a new inheritance, which, he told

me, made him pretty well off; and he decided to drain the pond. The operation took the whole of one summer: it horribly disfigured his place, and it afflicted the neighbourhood with the stench of slime that was now laid bare. One family whose place adjoined Stryker's were obliged to go away for weeks during the heaviest days of August, when the draining had become complete. Stryker, however, stayed and personally attended to the turtles, cutting off their heads himself; and he had men posted day and night at the places where they went to lay their eggs. At last someone complained to the Board of Health, and they made him fill up his pond. He was indignant with the town authorities and declared that he had not yet got all the turtles, some of which were still hiding in the mud; and he and his crew put in a mad last day combing the bottom with giant rakes.

The next spring the turtles reappeared, though at first there were only a few. Stryker came over to see me and told me a harrowing story. He described how he had been sitting on his porch watching 'my finest pair of mallard, out with their new brood of young ones. They were still just like little fluffy balls, but they sailed along with that air they have of knowing that they're somebody special. From the moment that they can catch a water bug for themselves, they know that they're the lords of the pond. And I was just thinking how damn glad I was that no goblins were going to git them any more. Well, the phone rang and I went in to answer it, and when I came out again I distinctly had the impression that there were fewer ducks on the pond. So I counted them, and, sure enough, there was one duckling shy!' The next day another had vanished, and he had hired a man to watch the pond. Several snapping turtles were seen, but he had not succeeded in catching them. By the middle of the summer the casualties seemed almost as bad as before.

This time Mr Stryker decided to do a better job. He came to see me again and startled me by holding forth in a vein that recalled the pulpit. 'If God has created the mallard,' he said, 'a thing of beauty and grace, how can He allow these dirty filthy mud-turtles to prey upon His handiwork and destroy it?' 'He created the mud-turtles first,' I said. 'The reptiles came before the birds. And they survive with the strength God gave them. There is no instance on record of God's intervention in the affairs of any animal species lower in the scale than man.' 'But if the Evil triumphs there,' said Stryker, 'it may triumph everywhere, and we must fight it with every weapon in our power!' 'That's the Manichaean heresy,' I replied. 'It is an error to assume that the Devil is contending on equal terms with God and that the fate of the world is in doubt.' 'I'm not sure of that sometimes,' said Stryker, and I noticed that his little bright eyes seemed to dim in a curious way as if he were drawing into himself to commune with some private fear. 'How do we know that some of His lowest creations aren't beginning to get out of hand and clean up on the higher ones?'

He decided to poison the turtles, and he brushed up, as he told me, on his chemistry. The result, however, was all too devastating. The chemicals he put into the water wiped out not only the turtles, but also all the other animals and most of the vegetation in the pond. When his chemical analysis showed that the water was no longer tainted, he put back the ducks again, but they found so little to eat that they presently flew away and ceased to frequent the place. In the meantime, some new ones that had come there had died from the poisoned water. One day, as Asa M. Stryker was walking around his estate, he encountered a female snapping turtle unashamedly crawling in the direction of the pond. She had obviously just been laying her eggs. He had had the whole of his place closed in with a fence of thick-meshed wire which went down a foot into the ground (I had asked him why he didn't have the pond rather than the whole estate thus enclosed, and he had explained that this would have made it impossible for him to look at the ducks from the porch); but turtles must have got in through the gate when it was open or they must have been in hiding all the time. Stryker was, as the English say, livid, and people became a little afraid of him because they thought he was getting cracked.

II

That afternoon he paid a visit to a man named Clarence Latouche, whose place was just behind Stryker's. Latouche was a native of New Orleans, and he worked in the advertising business. When Asa Stryker arrived, he was consuming a tall Scotch highball, unquestionably not his first; and he tried to make Stryker have a drink in the hope that it would relieve his tension. But 'I don't use it thanks,' said Stryker, and he started his theological line about the ducks and the snapping turtles. Clarence Latouche, while Stryker was talking, dropped his eyes for a moment to the wing collar and the large satin cravat which his neighbour always wore in the country and which were evidently associated in his mind with some idea, acquired in a provincial past, of the way for a 'man of means' to dress. It seemed to him almost indecent that this desperate moral anxiety should agitate a being like Stryker.

'Well,' he commented in his easy way when he had listened for a few minutes, 'if the good God can't run the universe, where He's supposed to be the supreme authority, without letting in the forces of Evil, I don't see how we poor humans in our weakness can expect to do any better with a few acres of Hecate County, where we're at the mercy of all the rest of creation.' 'It *ought* to be possible,' said Stryker. 'And I say it damn well *shall* be possible!' 'As I see it,' said Clarence Latouche – again, and again unsuccessfully, offering Stryker a drink – 'you're faced with a double problem. On the one hand, you've got to get rid of the snappers; and, on the other

86

hand, you've got to keep the ducks. So far you haven't been able to do either. Whatever measure you take, you lose the ducks and you can't kill the snappers. Now it seems to me, if you'll pardon my saying so, that you've overlooked the real solution – the only and, if you don't mind my saying so, the obvious way to deal with the matter.' 'I've been over the whole ground,' said Stryker, growing more tense and turning slightly hostile under pressure of his pent-up passion, 'and I doubt whether there's any method that I haven't considered with the utmost care.' 'It seems to me,' said Clarence Latouche in his gentle Louisiana voice, 'that, going about the thing as you have been, you've arrived at a virtual *impasse* and that you ought to approach the problem from a totally different angle. If you do that, you'll find it perfectly simple' – Stryker seemed about to protest fiercely, but Clarence continued in a vein of mellow alcoholic explaining: 'The trouble is, as I see it, that up to now you've been going on the assumption that you ought to preserve the birds at the expense of getting rid of the turtles. Why not go on the opposite assumption: that you ought to work at cultivating the snappers? Shoot the ducks when they come around, and eat them – that is, when the law permits it' – Mr Stryker raised a clenched fist and started up in inarticulate anger – 'or if you don't want to do that, shoo them off. Then feed up the snappers on raw meat. Snappers are right good eating, too. We make soup out of 'em down in my part of the country.'

Mr Stryker stood speechless for such a long moment that Clarence was afraid, he said afterwards, that his neighbour would fall down in a fit; and he got up and patted him on the shoulder and exerted all his tact and charm. 'All I can say,' said Stryker, as he was going out the door, 'is that I can't understand your attitude. Right is Right and Wrong is Wrong, and you have to choose between them!'

'I've never been much of a moralist,' said Clarence, 'and I dare say my whole point of view is a low and pragmatical one.'

III

Stryker spent a troubled and restless night – so he afterwards told Clarence Latouche; but he got up very early, as he always did, to go hunting for breakfasting turtles, which he lured with pieces of steak. He would scoop them up with a net, and this morning he paused over the first one he caught before he cut off its head. He scrutinized it with a new curiosity, and its appearance enraged him afresh: he detested its blunt sullen visage, its thick legs with their outspread claws, and its thick and thorny-toothed tail that it could not even pull into its shell as other turtles did. It was not even a genuine turtle: *Chelydra serpentina* they called it, because it resembled a snake, and it crawled like a huge lizard. He baited it with a stick: it snapped with a sharp popping sound. As he held the beast up in his net, in the limpid morning air which was brimming the world like a tide, it looked, with its feet dripping slime, its dull shell that resembled a sunken log, as fetid, as cold and as dark as the bottom of the pond itself; and he was almost surprised at the gush of blood when he sawed away the head. What good purpose, he asked himself in horror, could such a creature serve? Subterranean, ugly and brutal – with only one idea in its head, or rather one instinct in its nature: to seize and hold down its prey. The turtle had snapped at the hoop of the net, and even now that its head was severed, its jaws were still holding on.

Stryker pried the head off the net and tossed it into the water; another turtle rose to snatch it. Then why not turn the tables on Nature? Why not prey on what preyed on us? Why not exploit the hideous mud-turtle, as his friend from the South had suggested? Why not devour him daily in the form of turtle soup? And if one could not eat soup every day, why not turn him into an object of commerce? Why not make the public eat him? Let the turtles create economic, instead of kill-ing aesthetic, value! He snickered at what seemed to him a fantasy; but he returned to Clarence Latouche's that day in one of his expansive moods that rather gave Clarence the creeps.

'Nothing easier!' cried Latouche, much amused – his advertising copy irked him, and he enjoyed an opportunity to burlesque it. 'You know, the truth is that a great big proportion of the canned turtle soup that's sold is made out of snapping turtles, but that isn't the way they advertise it. If you advertise it frankly as snapper, it will look like something brand-new, and all you'll need is the snob appeal to put it over on the can-opening public. There's a man canning rattlesnakes in Florida, and it ought to be a lot easier to sell snappers. All you've got to do up here in the North to persuade people to buy a product, is to convince them that there's some kind of social prestige attached to it – and all you'd have to do with your snappers would be to create the impression that a good ole white-haired darky with a beaming smile used to serve turtle soup to Old Massa. All you need is a little smart advertising and you can have as many people eating snapper as are eating [he named a popular canned salmon], which isn't even nutritious like snapper is – they make it out of the sweepings from a tyre factory. – I tell you what I'll do,' he said, carried away by eloquence and whisky, 'you organize a turtle farm and I'll write you some copy free. You can pay me when and if you make money.'

Mr Stryker went back to his pond, scooped out two of the largest snappers, and that evening tried some snapping-turtle soup, which seemed to him surprisingly savoury. Then he looked up the breeding of turtles, about which, in the course of his war with them, he had already come to know a good deal. He replenished his depleted pond with turtles brought from other ponds, for which he paid the country boys a dime apiece, and at the end of a couple of years he had such a population of snappers that he had to stock the pond with more frogs.

Clarence Latouche helped him launch his campaign and, as he had promised, wrote the copy for it. There had already appeared at that time a new device, of which Clarence had been one of the originators, for putting over the products of the meat-packers. The animals were represented as gratified and even gleeful at the idea of being eaten. You saw pictures of manicured and be-ribboned porkers capering and smirking at the prospect of being put up in glass jars as sausages, and of steers in white aprons and chefs' hats that offered you their own sizzling beefsteaks. Clarence Latouche converted the snapping turtle into a genial and lovable creature, who became a familiar character to the readers of magazines and the passengers on subway trains. He was pictured as always smiling, with a twinkle in his wise old eye, and he had always some pungent saying which smacked of the Southern backwoods, and which Clarence had great fun writing. As for the plantation angle, that was handled in a novel fashion. By this time the public had been oversold on Old Massa with the white moustaches, so Clarence invented a lady, lovely, highbred and languid like Mrs St Clare in *Uncle Tom's Cabin*, who had to be revived by turtle soup. 'Social historians tell us,' one of the advertisements ran, 'that more than 70 per cent of the women of the Old South suffered from anaemia or phthisis [here there was an asterisk referring to a note, which said "Tuberculosis"]. Turtle soup saved the sweethearts and mothers of a proud and gallant race. The rich juices of the Alabama snapping turtle, fed on a special diet handed down from the time of Jefferson and raised on immaculate turtle farms famous for a century in the Deep South, provide the vital calories so often lacking in the modern meal.' The feminine public were led to identify themselves with the lady and to feel that they could enjoy a rich soup and yet remain slender and snooty. The advertisement went on to explain that many women still suffered, without knowing it, from anaemia and t.b., and that a regular consumption of turtle soup could cure or ward off these diseases.

Deep South Snapper Soup became an immense success; and the demand was presently stimulated by putting three kinds on the market: Deep South Snapper Consommé, Deep South Snapper Tureen (Extra Thick), and Deep South Snapper Medium Thick, with Alabama Whole-Flour Noodles.

Stryker had to employ more helpers, and he eventually built a small cannery, out of sight of the house, on his place. The turtles were raised in shallow tanks, in which they were easier to catch and control.

IV

Mr Stryker, who had not worked for years at anything but his struggle with the turtles, turned out to be startlingly able as a businessman and industrial organizer. He kept down his working crew, handled his correspondence himself, brow-beat a small corps of salesmen, and managed to make a very large profit. He went himself to the city relief bureaux and unerringly picked out men who were capable and willing to work but not too independent or intelligent, and he put over them his gardener as foreman. He would begin by lending these employees money, and he boarded and fed them on the place – so that they found themselves perpetually in debt to him. He took on as a secretary a school-teacher who had lost her job. A plain woman of middle age, she had suddenly had a baby by a middle-aged Italian mechanic who worked in a crossroads garage. Asa Stryker boarded the mother and agreed to pay board for the baby at a place he selected himself. As the business began to prosper, this secretary came to handle an immense amount of correspondence and other matters, but Stryker always criticized her severely and never let her feel she was important.

He had managed to accomplish all this without ever giving

people the impression that he was particularly interested in the business; yet he had always followed everything done with a keen and remorseless attention that masked itself under an appearance of impassivity. Every break for a market was seized at once; every laxity of his working staff was pounced on. And his attitude toward the turtles themselves had now changed in a fundamental fashion. He had come to admire their alertness and toughness; and when he took me on a tour of his tanks, he would prod them and make them grip his stick, and then laugh proudly when they would not let go as he banged them against the concrete.

Clarence Latouche himself, who had invented Snapper Tureen, presently began to believe that he was a victim of Stryker's sharp dealing. At the time when the business was beginning to prosper, they had signed an agreement which provided that Clarence should get 10 per cent; and he now felt that he ought to have a bigger share – all the more since his casual habits were proving fatal to his job at the agency. He had been kept for the brilliant ideas which he was some-times able to contribute, but he had lately been drinking more heavily and it had been hinted that he might be fired. He was the kind of New Orleans man who, extraordinarily charming in youth, becomes rather overripe in his twenties and goes to pieces with an astonishing rapidity. In New Orleans this would not have been noticed; but in the North he had never been quite in key and he was now feeling more ill at ease and more hostile to his adopted environment. He had been carry-ing on an affair with a married woman, whom he had expected to divorce her husband and marry him; but he had become rather peevish with waiting, and she had decided that a divorce was a good deal of trouble, and that it was perhaps not entirely true that his drinking was due to her failure to marry him. Lately Clarence had taken to brooding on Stryker, whom he had been finding it rather difficult to see, and he had come to the conclusion that the latter was devious as well as sordid, and that he had been misrepresenting to Clarence the amount of profit he made.

One Sunday afternoon, at last, when Clarence had been sitting alone with a succession of tall gin fizzes, he jumped up suddenly, strode out the door, cut straight through his grounds to the fence which divided his property from Stryker's, climbed over it with inspired agility, and made a beeline for Stryker's house, purposely failing to follow the drive and stepping through the flower-beds. Stryker came himself to the door with a look that, if Clarence had been sober, he would have realized was apprehensive; but when he saw who the visitor was, he greeted him with a special cordiality, and ushered him into his study. With his highly developed awareness, he had known at once what was coming.

This study, which Clarence had never seen, as he rarely went to Stryker's house, was a disorderly and darkish place. It was characteristic of Stryker that his desk should seem littered and neglected, as if he were not really in touch with his affairs; and there was dust on the books in his bookcase, drably bound and unappetizing volumes on zoological and chemical subjects. Though it was daytime, the yellow-brown shades were pulled three-quarters down. On the desk and on the top of the bookcase stood a number of handsome stuffed ducks that Stryker had wished to preserve.

Stryker sat down at his desk and offered Clarence a cigarette. Instead of protesting at once that Clarence's demands were impossible, as he had done on previous occasions, he listened with amiable patience. 'I'm going to go into the whole problem and put things on a different basis as soon as business slackens up in the spring. So I'd rather you'd wait till then, if you don't mind. We had a hard time filling the orders even before this strike began, and now I can hardly get the work done at all. They beat up two of my men yesterday, and they're threatening to make a raid on the factory. I've had to have the whole place guarded.' (The breeding ponds and the factory, which were situated half a mile away, had been enclosed by a wire fence.) Clarence had forgotten the strike, and he realized that he *had* perhaps come at a rather inopportune time. 'I can't attend to a reorganization,' Stryker went on to explain – 'which is what we've got to have at this point – till our labour troubles are settled and things have slowed up a bit. There ought to be more in this business for both of us,' he concluded, with a businessman's smile, 'and I won't forget your co-operative attitude when we make a new arrangement in the spring.'

The tension was thus relaxed, and Stryker went on to address Clarence with something like friendly concern. 'Why don't you have yourself a vacation?' he suggested. 'I've noticed you were looking run-down. Why don't you go South for the winter? Go to Florida or someplace like that. It must be tough for a Southerner like you to spend this nasty part of the year in the North. I'll advance you the money, if you need it.' Clarence was half tempted, and he began to talk to Stryker rather freely about the idiocies of the advertising agency and about the two aunts and a sister whom he had to support in Baton Rouge. But in the course of the conversation, as his eye escaped from Stryker's gaze, which he felt as uncomfortably intent in the gaps between sympathetic smiles, it lit on some old chemical apparatus, a row of glass test-tubes and jars, which had presumably been carried along from Stryker's early career as a teacher; and he remembered – though the steps of his reasoning may have been guided, as he afterwards sometimes thought, by a delusion of persecution that had been growing on his in recent months – he remembered the deaths, at intervals, of Stryker's well-to-do relatives. His eye moved on to the mounted ducks, with their rich but rather lustreless colours. He had always been half-conscious with the other of his own superior grace of appearance and manner and speech, and had sometimes felt that Stryker admired it; and now as he contemplated Stryker, at ease in his turbid room, upended, as it were, behind his desk, with a broad expanse of plastron and a rubbery craning neck, regarding him with small bright eyes set back in the brownish skin beyond a prominent snoutlike formation of which the nostrils were sharply in evidence – as Clarence confronted Stryker, he felt first a fantastic suspicion, then a sudden unnerving certainty.

Unhurriedly he got up to go and brushed away Stryker's regret that – since it was Sunday and the cook's day out – he was unable to ask him to dinner. But his nonchalance now disguised panic: it was hideously clear to him why Stryker had suggested his taking this trip. He wouldn't go, of course, but what then? Stryker would be sure to get him if he didn't take some prompt action. In his emotion, he forgot his hat and did not discover it till they had reached the porch. He stepped back into the study alone, and on an impulse took down from its rack on the wall the rifle with which Stryker, in the earlier days, had gone gunning for snapping turtles. He opened the screen door. Stryker was standing on the porch. As he looked around, Clarence shot him.

The cook was out; only the gates were guarded; and Clarence had arrived at Stryker's by taking the back cut through the grounds. Nobody heard the shot. The suspicion all fell on the foreman, who had his own long-standing grievances and had organized the current strike. He had already had to go into hiding to escape from his boss's thugs, and after the murder he disappeared.

Clarence decided soon that he would sell his Hecate County place and travel for a year in Europe, which he had always wanted to see. But just after he had bought his passage, the war with Hitler started, and prevented him from getting off – an ironic disappointment he said, for a smart advertising man who had been speculating in snapping turtles.

He had dissociated himself from the soup business, and he went to live in southern California, where, on his very much dwindled income, he is said to be drinking himself to death. He lives under the constant apprehension that the foreman may be found by the police, and that he will then have to confess his own guilt in order to save an innocent man – because Clarence is the soul of honour – so that Stryker may get him yet.

A. L. BARKER

A. L. BARKER (1918–   ) left school at sixteen and started work in a city office. She worked for a literary agent and then, after the War, joined the BBC in 1949. By then her first book of short stories Innocents (1947) *from which the strange story 'The Doll' is taken had been published. Since then she has written several more collections including* Lost upon the Roundabouts, *and more recently* Femina Real (1971). *Miss Barker has also published several novels:* A Case Examined (1965), The Middling (1967), John Brown's Body (1969), *and* Source of Embarrassment (1974). *She is a writer whose fiction is much admired by her fellow writers, has won literary prizes, but has not been as widely read as it deserves.*

The Doll

She felt inclined to dress up. It was the day which prompted her, a day – had she known it – very like herself. For she was one of those creatures who carry such weather with them, who conjure up and are themselves conjured by blue, guileless skies, avuncular sun and twists of pink almond blossom.

She tied up her hair with a green ribbon; the bow was startling among bright bronze curls which she had forgotten to comb. Ribbon was hardly enough; she needed flowers, posies of them, and perhaps a veil to make her mysterious. Mysterious in her own right, she was not. Her eyes were wide, blue and credulous like a kitten's, her cheek pink and white and curved as the most unambiguous petal. Wishes, she had long since learned, only reach their ideal conclusion in fairy-tales, but she had always kept her answer ready in case fortune should ever put her into the way of asking in the proper quarters. She would wish to be dark and disastrous as an odalisque, with raven hair, long eyes and bangles from wrist to elbow.

In the meantime, she had decided on flowers, and since she had none of her own, she went to her mother's room.

As usual, there was the wild skelter of brushes, combs, pots and perfumes scattered over the dressing-table. The powder-puff was there in a drift of peach-coloured pollen, and a stub of petunia lipstick beside it. Sighing happily she went in and closed the door. She had been away and not until now, on finding her mother's room as it always was, did she feel she had come home again.

Her mother was out shopping; she had time and to spare; it would be as if she had never gone away.

In the top drawer of the dressing-table were scarves, gloves, stockings and handkerchiefs whirled together as by some centrifugal force. There were, too, posies of artificial flowers, camellias, violets, roses, silk poppies, anemones and – incongruous with her sophisticated mother – a bunch of velvet buttercups and daisies. Something white tucked down one side of the drawer, caught her attention. She drew it out and saw that it was the last birthday card she had sent her mother.

She always chose for other people the kind of birthday cards she herself loved best to receive; glossy pictures of kittens, puppies and caskets of riotous flowers. Her mother loathed them; had she known that, she would have been as shocked as if a sunset had been reviled. To her, the beauty of the clouds was commensurate with the beauty of the shiny postcards.

On the back of the card, in her own apple-round writing, she read: 'To Mummy, always many happy returns – from Alice.'

From Alice. She stroked a finger over the glossy surface. Just Alice. Not even Alicia. Could one be dark and disastrous with a name like that? One could only try.

She fastened camellias in her hair, buttercups at her neck and a wisp of fine Spanish veiling wound over her eyes and forehead. Searchingly she peered out through the cobweb and found that she looked a little like an odd French poupée a little like a chocolate-box cameo, but most of all like her own self decked with flowers and black veiling.

Dissatisfied, she took off the flowers, put a round feathered toque on her head and in a moment of inspiration, tied the veiling round it and under her chin. The effect was miraculous. She looked modern, she looked mischievous, she looked grown-up.

Alice went and sat down on the bed. She folded her hands in her lap and rested a moment. She had been ill and she could not stand up for long without feeling tired. But with the hat and the veil she had just achieved something, she rested on these, her laurels.

The something which Alice had achieved – it came to most people without their knowing or striving for it. Perhaps one day it would come to Alice. Until it did, she would see it everywhere but in herself. She would try to imitate it, borrowing its stance, its tone of voice, its way with a teaspoon, its manner of crossing the feet in company. Alice called it 'being grown-up' and she believed it could be put on all at once with a hat, or spindle-heeled shoes or fox furs.

After a moment she was tired of sitting still, she got up and went to the window, walking stiffly from the hips as she had noticed a friend of her mother's doing. Down below in the green handkerchief of a garden she could see a shining new pram with bright chromium wheels. She leaned on the sill and considered it.

She had been ill, weeks ago she had been very ill – languidly Alice tucked away a curl – she had almost died. Immense, the power in that near negative achievement. Not that she knew anything about it; some part of herself had made the decision for her and almost carried it out. Since then she had been the most important person in the house.

Since then, too, there had been the pram with the doll in it. As long as Alice could remember, they had given her a present after she had been ill. She reckoned on her fingers – a box of bricks after mumps, a rocking-horse after measles, three brown bears after whooping-cough and a tricycle when she had her tonsils out. Now there was this.

It was more ambitious than any of the other presents. Perhaps that was appropriate, for her illness had been more ambitious. The doll they had brought to her in hospital. Alice forgot the grown-up hat and breathed on the window-pane; with her finger she drew two circles, one above the other, with dots for eyes and waistcoat buttons.

She remembered how disappointed she had been at sight of

the doll. She could only suppose it was a humorous kind of doll; they should have known by now that she did not like humorous dolls. She liked a doll which could be wheeled out proudly and which other people could envy. When, Alice asked herself with chagrin, would she ever be able to wheel *this* doll out with the hope of rousing pride in herself or envy in others? Curiosity, perhaps, might make someone look twice at it.

But she was glad she hadn't let them see her disappointment, for people had feelings like egg-shells – it was her belief that once damaged they could never be whole again. She sighed, remembering how polite she had been and how willing that the doll should be put aside. She was still willing, and as she did not like to pretend in earnest, she waited now for a time when it could be put aside for good.

Still wearing the hat and veil, Alice went downstairs, walking with one hand on the banisters and the other on her hip. There was nothing provocative in her pose, it was not a flamboyant swagger she acquired or sought to acquire. It was her honest conception of poise. By the time she reached the bottom of the stairs she was hungry and had forgotten it.

There was a jar of clover honey in the cupboard; she cut two slices of new bread, spread honey on each and sat on the floor in a lozenge of sunlight. A pale sticky bead dropped on to the veiling under her chin as she ate.

The moment came when she licked the last sweetness from her fingers and found there was nothing much to consider except her own rather thin legs stretched out straight before her. The feather toque had slipped far back, curls escaped from it and tumbled on her neck, bringing the green ribbon with them. The pink in her candid cheeks deepened with contentment and the warmth of the sun.

She must have fallen asleep because the crying awoke her. But first it wound itself into a dream, it became the thin crying of a bird in spaces huge as only the space of dreams can be. She awoke in a terror of loneliness and found that the high desolate cry of the bird was still with her under the blue sky and the sprigged almond trees.

Alice stood up, chilled. She knew where the cry came from, yet she pretended – abjectly she pretended to herself – that she did not know. She went upstairs, she took off the hat and veiling, she untied the ribbon and combed her hair. She smoothed her dress, she even gathered together the few crumbs which had fallen from her breakfast tray that morning. The crying went on.

She hurried into the bathroom to clean her teeth. She could hear the wailing above the sound of running water and now her knowledge of her own deceit was abysmal. Slowly, very slowly, she went out into the garden.

Someone was coming along the road. It was the postman. She ran gladly to him and took a letter; he said as she turned away, 'Your baby's crying.'

'Yes,' said Alice. 'Yes, I know.'

She stood and watched him go with all the intensity of a castaway who sees a ship pass his desert island. Then she went to the pram, seized it by the handle and rocked it commandingly. The crying did not stop. Alice wheeled the pram to and fro on the grass, but now the wail had a weak, strangled sound. She pushed down the hood and gingerly held back the covers.

It was a tiny head, puckered like a crab-apple and turning desperately from side to side on its frilled pillow. The eyes were closed, the small nostrils were pinched shut, the minute fists were curled; only the mouth was open to express a conviction of endless, immeasurable sorrow. Round and hot it had always looked, but never, surely, had it been such a deep, congested crimson?

'Stop!' cried Alice sharply. 'You'd better stop!'

It took no notice, that thin lonely wail went on, beginning and ending on the same note, declaring again and again the uselessess and the tyranny of effort. Each fist shook a little, not in defence but as the contribution of the mute to the articulate sorrow.

Alice turned away in exasperation. She went and picked the head of a daffodil – something she would never have done had she not been so disturbed. The yellow petals dropped one by one at her feet. And then the crying changed, it grew breathless, shuddering; there were short sharp silences not of peace but of a desperate and fruitless labour.

Alice went back to the pram. The tiny dark red face had now a tinge of blue in it, no sound except a faint spiderish rustle came from the wide open mouth.

Something happened to Alice. She flung back the coverlets, picked up the child and laid it against her shoulder with the deftness of one who had dealt with generations of dolls. Her free hand – as in a remembered ritual – gently patted the baby's back. She walked up and down, murmuring to it, her body relaxed for its comfort, tensed for its utmost protection. The wailing died, the dark red cheek cooled beside her own.

Alice was leaning over her son in his pram when her mother returned from shopping. She rounded swiftly at the click of the gate.

'Do be quiet, mother,' she said. 'I've just got him off to sleep.'

ANGUS WILSON

ANGUS WILSON (1913–) Born in England, brought up in South Africa, and educated at Westminster and Oxford, his professional life was spent until 1955 as a member of the British Museum Library staff, where he held the post of Assistant Keeper, Department of Printed Books, and thereafter as Professor of English Literature at the University of East Anglia. 'What do Hippos Eat?' was first published in The Listener, *and subsequently in his second collection of short stories,* Such Darling Dodos (1950). *He is a novelist of the first importance, and is equally a master of the short story. A novelist must often wait for his reputation to grow before his short stories are published. Angus Wilson is unusual in that his first two publications were collections of short stories.*

What do Hippos Eat?

She seemed such a little bit of a thing as she peered through the railings at the huge, cumbrous bison, her neat boyish head of short-cut, tight red curls such a contrast to the matted chocolate wool that lay in patches around the beast's long, mournful features. 'Ginger for pluck' Maurice always called her, and indeed her well-knit little figure and firm stance were redolent of determination and cheek, and cried out her virtues as a real good pal, her Dead End Kid appeal that went through to the heart.

'My! My!' she said to the bison, 'someone forgot to bring his comb.' She was such a round-eyed urchin that one felt almost surprised when she did not put out her tongue.

Maurice smiled paternally and fingered his little grey first-world-war moustache. 'How would you like to have a couple of rounds in the ring with that?' he asked laughing.

'Oh! I'd take it on all right,' she said, and gave him one of her funny straight looks. She had only two roles with men – tomboy and good scout – even they were very alike, except that the good scout was full of deep, silent understanding and could hold her drink.

Maurice guffawed, 'My God! I believe you would. Size means nothing to you.' His admiration was perfectly genuine, for under his ostentatious virility he was a physically timorous man with a taste for the brutal. As he looked appraisingly at her slender shoulders and tight little breasts, he felt wonderfully protective and sentimental. All the same it irked him that he wasn't getting on faster with his scheme. It was true, he reflected, that he hadn't paid a sausage out in rent for the last two months and she'd cashed two stumers for him without batting an eyelid when they came back 'R.D.'; but now that he'd turned fifty-five he wanted a more secure berth than that. The truth was that Maurice had experienced some unpleasant bouts of giddiness in the mornings recently, and his heart – he called it 'the old ticker' even to himself – often missed a beat when he climbed upstairs. Under such circumstances, a partnership in the boarding house – it was his name for legalized use of her capital – would just suit him, with a liberal supply of pocket money for the 'dogs'. Earls Court wasn't exactly the neighbourhood he would have chosen, indeed, when he remembered his brief residence in Clarges Street, now seen in retrospect as lasting for years, he felt shamed that he should have sunk so low, but he had known too much of Camden Town and the York Road, Waterloo, in the interval not to count his blessings while they lasted. He was, in fact, worn out with schemes and lies and phoney deals, he slept badly and his nerves were giving way. Temporary setbacks made him act, as now, precipitately.

'It's grand to see you enjoying yourself, Greta,' he said. 'You ought to be having lots of fun whilst you're still young. It's a damned shame the way you have to work. You had a hard enough life as a kid, God knows, and now this blasted house hanging round your neck. It's too much even for your heavyweight shoulders,' and he laughed.

Greta stuck out her chin, 'I had my fun all right,' she said. 'You don't have to be rich to enjoy life as a kid.'

'Oh, I know,' Maurice replied, with a smile as though she had been referring to hopscotch in the back alley. 'You can take it on the chin all right, I'll say that for you. But all the same,' he continued with a sigh, 'I'd give my right hand to have known you when I still had a bit of money. *I'd* have put an end to all these worries.'

Greta had decided not to notice Maurice's remarks for a few moments, so she turned to watch a scarlet ibis wading in the pool behind them.

'Aren't you a lucky bird not to be a hat?' she asked. She had her special brand of humour – the gang at the local called it 'Greta's dopey jokes'. Then, 'You're my only money worry, Maurice Legge,' she said, her Manchester accent more emphasized than usual, 'and what are you going to do about *that*?'

Self-pity and suppressed anger brought beads of sweat to his temples and he mopped them with the silk handkerchief which he kept in his cuff – an old ex-officer habit, he was always careful to explain. Two pictures flashed before him in quick succession. First, the young ex-subaltern, a possible for the Harlequins; handsome, easy-going; a man to whom stockbrokers offered £2,000-a-year jobs on his social contacts alone. Then the other picture – still a handsome man, old and tired now, but unmistakably a gentleman for all the doubtful shifts into which life had forced him – he bent before the cheap snubs and insults of a common little creature, whom the ex-subaltern would not have noticed in a crowd. He could almost hear the commentator say, 'Look upon this picture and on *this*,' and his eyes filled with tears. This cinematographic representation of life had grown on him in middle age. It was not a surprising phenomenon, since his days were passed in a highly coloured histrionic blur. He would move from Prince's to the Cri, from the Cri to the Troc, from the Troc to Oddenino's, trying with a closely-knit web of circumstantial narrative to pull off complicated deals or, at the very least, to cadge a drink from some toughly sentimental whisky-soaking Colonial or American. In the intervals of this 'work', he went to the 'pictures' or sat before the gasfire of his bed-sitting room working out large betting schemes which he had not the capital to realize, or reading cheap thrillers. Past, present, and future, truth and lies, all moved before him in short, vivid, dramatic scenes that merged into a background mist of anxiety, imagined grandeur and sticky sentiment. But behind it all was a certain hard core of determination to survive. It was this that made him swallow Greta's snub and turn to the buffaloes.

'Nice mild-looking fellows, you would say about those, wouldn't you?' he asked. Greta looked at their large, brown calf's eyes and their shapely horns, and nodded.

'How wrong you'd be,' said Maurice. 'I shall never forget once up country from Nairobi going through a village after buffalo had stampeded. Not a pleasant sight at all. Harry Brand was with me and I've never seen a chap turn so green. "So help me God, Maurice," he said, "I shall have to call it a day and turn back." Funny thing, really, because he was a beefy sort of cove. But you remember him, anyhow.'

Greta shook her head. 'Oh yes you do, darling,' said Maurice, 'great red-faced fellow we met one evening outside the Plaza.' Greta looked puzzled but denied it. 'I'm sure you did,' Maurice went on. Then he added thoughtfully, 'But wait a minute though, perhaps you're right. Yes, you are. I was with Dolly.' And, glad to have checked this point, he returned to Kenya with renewed ardour.

Greta listened to his stories with rapt attention. However her business acumen and natural hardness might protect her against his wilder financial schemes, her pride and delight in his recounted exploits were for once in her life quite unselfconsciously childlike. His attraction as a gentleman was enhanced for her by the cosmopolitan background which every day of their intimacy revealed a little more. She felt, more justly than she realized, that it was an authentication of all that the films had hinted to her. The digressions, irrelevant ramifications, and long-winded checks of memory in which Maurice indulged might have been expected to bore his listeners, but strangely enough they were exactly the features which finally convinced the sceptical, banishing suspicions of glibness and lending realism to art. To Greta they were the supreme pleasure, for they seemed somehow to involve her own participation in these exciting adventures. After all she had, it seemed, only just missed meeting Harry Brand outside the Plaza. For Maurice himself they formed a reassurance which his self-confidence badly needed. He had told so many stories for so many years, truth and fiction were so inextricably mixed, that to check a new falsehood by a poorly remembered old one made him feel that in some way truth must be involved somewhere.

As they walked into the Lion House Maurice felt his confidence returning. He was ready for any audience. And there, gazing at the Siberian tiger, an audience awaited him – an elderly solicitor and his wife, a working-class woman with two small children. Maurice began to talk to Greta in a voice pitched loudly enough for the others to hear.

'Siberian tiger, eh?' he said. 'A present from our not such dear friends the Russians. He's a beautiful creature, though. Never had any experience with them myself, but I should think they might be very ugly customers. Don't you agree, sir?' he asked the solicitor, who replied embarrassedly, 'Yes, yes, I should imagine so.'

'No,' said Maurice loudly and self deprecatingly. 'I've only run across this chap's Indian cousin who's altogether smaller fry. Most of this stuff about man-eaters, you know, is a lot of nonsense. No tiger turns to human flesh until he's too old to hold his own in the jungle.'

'Do you hear that, Billy?' said the woman to her son.

'Oh, yes,' Maurice continued, 'all these round-ups of tigers for important people, makes you laugh if you know about it, half the poor blighters can hardly stand up with old age. So if anyone asks you to a tiger shoot, laddy,' he said to the boy, 'you can be sure of bringing your mother back a nice new rug.'

'There you are, Billy,' said the woman, 'you hear what the gentleman says,' and everyone laughed.

Greta felt so proud of Maurice. He looked so handsome, despite all his wrinkles and pouches, and the line of his arm appeared so strong and manly as he gripped the rail in front of him, that she longed to take his hand in hers and to stroke it.

He had told her so often, however, that physical caresses in public were 'just not done', and she was able now to check herself in time. Greta was both anxious and quick to learn as she climbed up the economic ladder, and she felt it was one of the great advantages of her relations with Maurice that he could teach her so much. She no longer said 'serviette' or dropped her shoes off under restaurant tables. She never went out now without gloves – Maurice's ideas of polite behaviour belonged rather to his early years – but she also no longer blew into them when she took them off. She could hardly guess that he had mixed little with respectable people of any class for over fifteen years, and thus she was able to retain many of her humorous phrases – 'he's a smell on the landing to me' was a favourite – without qualms, for Maurice greeted them with a smile. She was jealous sometimes of his larking with waitresses, but he told her not to be suburban, and in any case she felt ready to forgive anything as she watched him finger the knot of his old school tie whilst he studied the menu, and heard him refer to her as 'Madam' when he finally gave the order.

As the keeper passed the tiger cage with a bucket of dung Maurice asked him which the biggest lion was now and how many pounds of meat the black leopard consumed in a day. He was one of the older keepers and received Maurice's officer-to-batman manner in a more friendly spirit than was often the case these days. Soon the whole party was being taken behind the scenes to watch a puma cross one of the little bridges to its outdoor cage. Greta felt quite queenly when she saw the respectful manner in which the keeper received Maurice's tip, and she attempted a new charming bow and smile as the party broke up. She even approved Maurice's giving sixpence to the two little children, though in general she did not care to spend her money too lavishly.

Maurice looked ten years younger as they walked away from the Lion House. He had always been interested in wild animals, felt a mastery over them that he lacked with men, and these boyish sensations combined with a genuine aesthetic feeling for their shape and colour were now reawakened. It was so seldom that he experienced any pleasure divorced from his own schemes and anxieties these days, and his body expanded and revelled in the carefree mood. He stroked the soft nose of the caribou as it pushed through the bars in quest of food. It was not, therefore, surprising that he felt little pleasure in Greta's urchin impudence when she gave the animal the raspberry. But he was too happy to comment on her vulgarity. For her, wild animals were an alarming and remote tribe, that once secured behind bars or in travelling circuses, could be treated as comic turns.

But Greta's thoughts were not, in any case, on the beasts, they were very much upon Maurice. She had seldom felt him so desirable, and it worried her to see the creases of his suit – so overcleaned and repaired – shine in the sunlight. She knew the pitiable state of his few underclothes and threadbare second suit as they reposed in the chest of drawers in a litter of important-looking papers, solicitors' letters, unpaid bills, and pawntickets – knew only too well, for in the first weeks of his failure to pay his rent she had searched in vain for any saleable articles. Though she could not allow him to handle her money since he was obviously so foolish about business, he *was* her man and she wanted him to look nice. She made up her mind to buy him a whole new outfit. She had done very well out of letting her rooms in the last few years and could afford to spend a little and still leave the good margin in the bank which represented respectability to her. Greta's realism had begun at sixteen as a waitress, Maurice's had never really got going: it was hardly an even match. In her greater sense of reality she was far clearer about what she did and did not want. She wanted a man, and the fact that he was twenty years older did not trouble her, for she liked experience. Nevertheless she did not want to tie herself to someone who might play fast and loose with her savings, nor even perhaps would she want that man at all when he had passed sixty. However if he was not to have her money he should certainly have a suit.

Greta's friendly thoughts, her increased desire for him, communicated themselves to Maurice and, added to his own happy mood, made him walk on air. Tips passed lavishly as they fed the sea-lions from the rocks – Greta screamed and jumped like a little girl as the shapely blubbery creatures flopped about her – gave honey to the brown bear – Maurice smiled in his old way as she cried 'Who's got a bear behind?' – how devil-may-care he was with a carefully selected snake coiled round his arm! The monkeys rather damped their ardour, for they were both united in their prudish disapproval of certain antics. But an incident in front of the spider monkey's cage finally broke up their happy mood. They were laughing delightedly as the monkeys snatched the bread they offered and swung away with feet, hands and tails alike, when a young couple approached the cage. In general Greta did not care for freaks and there was certainly something a bit cranky about the young woman's long, shapeless grey frock and the young man's corduroys and knapsack. They were, in fact, R.A.D.A. students at play. But their studied seriousness and carefully beautiful voices impressed Greta.

'Their movements *are* rather heavenly,' said the girl. 'Almost a ghostlike flitting.'

'It's immensely interesting that they should have developed prehensile tails,' said the boy, and seeing Greta watching him, he smiled the new shy smile he was developing to play Oswald in *Ghosts*. Greta was completely conquered and smiled back. Maurice began to talk loudly, but Greta frowned impatiently, for the boy was speaking again.

'You see they're really gibbons, at least I think so,' and he smiled shyly again, 'and yet they've developed prehensile tails as well as arms and legs for swinging. It's a complete vindication of Lamarck really.'

'You do find the oddest things interesting, darling,' said the girl. Greta felt so angry with her.

'You can always learn something if you keep your ears open,' she said and smiled again at the boy.

'Come along,' said Maurice impatiently. 'We don't want to watch these damned monkeys all day,' but Greta waited a few minutes before following.

They stood surveying the hideous flat features of the lion-faced baboon in angry silence. 'Why the hell you want to encourage that damned unwashed long-haired young swine,' said Maurice, 'I can't imagine.'

'Because,' replied Greta – she snapped like a turtle when she was annoyed – 'I'm willing to learn from others occasionally.'

'And you've got a hell of a lot to learn.'

'I fully appreciate the lessons,' Greta cried, 'and I hope you appreciate what I pay for them.'

Maurice's eyes narrowed with rage. 'What exactly do you mean by that?'

'Two months' rent. That's what I mean by that, Maurice Legge.' He raised his fist as though to hit her, and she ran from him, calling, 'You keep away from me.' An elderly woman turned to stare at them.

'I'll leave your bloody house tonight,' he shouted. 'You'll get your cheque tomorrow morning.'

'Yes,' said Greta, 'and it'll come back R.D. by the end of the week.'

'You little so-and-so,' Maurice cried; it was one of his favourite phrases. He was trembling with rage, but behind his anger he could see all his hopes crumbling. He felt completely at the end of his tether; a night on the streets at his age might finish him off. With a tremendous effort he controlled his temper.

'Don't let's be greater fools than God made us,' he said.

Greta watched his collapse with genuine pity, she felt more than ever determined to look after him. But first, like all men, he must be taught a lesson, a lesson for spoilt children. From the pages of her favourite woman's journal she recalled the advice, 'He will accept you at the price you put on yourself, so don't make yourself cheap' – it was not exactly the situation the editress had in mind, but it seemed to apply.

'No thank you, Maurice. I've had enough. We're friends if you like, but friends apart,' she felt very pleased with the phrase. Sturdy, jaunty, independent, she walked away from him, past the pelicans and the ravens, towards the tunnel. Maurice stood sullenly for a few minutes, then he ran after her. He saw her at the far end of the tunnel and shouted 'Greta! Greta!' until his ears were filled with the echoes. His heart was pounding heavily and his legs felt like lead. He noticed the flood level mark and wished he were under the waters. Greta stood and waited for him.

'I'm sorry, kiddie,' he said, 'I can't say more.'

'That's all right,' she replied, the perfect good scout. 'We'll say no more about it.'

They went slowly back through the tunnel to the tea-room.

The 'set' tea with watercress *ad lib* was like a children's picnic, as they laughed and teased away the memory of the angry outburst. Greta was determined to bring back Maurice's pleasure. She felt sure of her mastery now and was anxious to erase all trace of the events that had revealed it. She stuffed herself almost sick with bread and butter and buns, because he so delighted to tease her about her 'kid's appetite'. 'Greedy guts,' he said smiling, as she took a second helping of watercress. He was quite sentimental now, as he thought of where he would be without her generosity; she might not be a lady but she certainly had a heart of gold. Ever sanguine and tenacious, he began to consider new ways of putting his little scheme to her.

'Shall we have a dekko at the elephants and then make for home?' he asked.

As they passed through the tunnel once more, Greta thought

how alike all men are, just children really, and she purred as she thought how well she understood him. When they approached the pool where the orange-teethed coypus sat on the rocks, cleaning their whiskers, she began to sing, 'He's my guy. Heaven knows why I love him, but he's my guy.'

'There's your famous musquash coats,' said Maurice, pointing at the huge rats, with their wet, coarse bristles.

'I *should* believe you,' Greta cried. They were both delighted when he convinced her – he because she was such a funny ignorant little rascal, she because it really was surprising what he knew. 'Well I'll never have a musquash coat,' she cried, 'not from creatures with teeth like that.'

They watched the otter as it swam in crazy circles round its pool, trying ceaselessly to dig a way through the concrete sides down to the open sea. 'The way it keeps scrabbling,' said Greta, 'I should think it wanted to get out.' They both had to laugh at its antics.

When they reached the Elephant House Maurice asked the keeper if they could go to the back of the hippopotamus pool. He was quite a young Cockney who didn't respond to Maurice's manner at all.

'It's not usual,' he said. 'There's nothing to see, you know, that you can't see from here.'

'All the same,' replied Maurice, 'I'd like to take the lady round the back.'

'O.K. Colonel,' the boy said, winking across at Greta, 'but it's not the place I'd choose to take my girl friend.'

It was, indeed, most unattractive on closer inspection. The hot steam from the muddy water smelt abominably and the sides of the pool were slippery with slime. Every now and again the huge black forms would roll over, displacing ripples of brown foam-flecked water and malevolent eyes on the end of stalks would appear above the surface for a moment. Maurice offered the keeper half a crown.

'That's all right,' he said. 'You keep your money. I get

paid, you know.' It was most difficult to walk on the slimy surface and Maurice, who was exhausted from the afternoon's events, slipped and would have fallen had not the boy caught his arm. As he recovered his balance, he noticed Greta returning the keeper's amused smile. A moment later, a hippopotamus surfaced, blowing sprays of water from its great pink nostrils. Maurice's suit was flecked with mud.

'Sorry about that,' said the keeper.

But Greta begged him not to worry. 'It's a terrible old thing, anyway. I'm going to get him a new one tomorrow,' she explained.

Maurice felt his throat fill with rage, anger that almost blinded him. He put his hands on her hips and in a moment he would have pushed her into the thick vaporous water; then he suddenly realized that he had no idea what would happen. Hippos, he felt sure, were not carnivorous, but in their anger at the disturbance they might destroy her, and that would be the end of both of them, he reflected with bitter satisfaction. On the other hand, they might turn away from the floating Greta in disgust, in which case he would simply have mucked up all his schemes. He withdrew his hands in despair. Once again he had to control his fury.

Greta was most surprised when she felt his hands on her waist. How funny men were, she reflected, just when you thought you understood them, they did something unexpected like that. Maurice, who was always lecturing her for showing her affection in public! She was really rather touched by the gesture. All the same, she decided, it would be wiser not to notice it then. So turning her wide-eyed gaze up at him. 'What *do* hippos eat, darling?' she asked, in her childlike way.

TED HUGHES

TED HUGHES (1930–) Outstanding among contemporary poets, he has concentrated upon the natural world, in particular animals, and conveys in compressed, staccato images the sheer force that fills them and which he finds that they express. Animals are different. . . . They may be indifferent, alien, menacing, hostile. In his vision of nature he is close to D. H. Lawrence. In 'The Rain Horse' (from Wodwo, *1967) we find the stallion's potential realized imaginatively. But there is no softening of the inimical creature, by making him a symbol of human aspirations or a catalyst in human relationships, as D. H. Lawrence has done from a similar viewpoint and sensibility in a number of short stories. 'The Rain Horse' is more antiqu? myth than modern parable.* Wodwo, *from which it comes, is a sequence of poetry and prose, which we are asked by the author to read as a whole.*

The Rain Horse

As the young man came over the hill the first thin blowing of rain met him. He turned his coat-collar up and stood on top of the shelving rabbit-riddled hedgebank, looking down into the valley.

He had come too far. What had set out as a walk along pleasantly-remembered tarmac lanes had turned dreamily by gate and path and hedge-gap into a cross-ploughland trek, his shoes ruined, the dark mud of the lower fields inching up the trouser legs of his grey suit where they rubbed against each other. And now there was a raw, flapping wetness in the air that would be a downpour again at any minute. He shivered, holding himself tense against the cold.

This was the view he had been thinking of. Vaguely, without really directing his walk, he had felt he would get the whole thing from this point. For twelve years, whenever he had recalled this scene, he had imagined it as it looked from here. Now the valley lay sunken in front of him, utterly deserted, shallow, bare fields, black and sodden as the bed of an ancient lake after the weeks of rain.

Nothing happened. Not that he had looked forward to any very transfiguring experience. But he had expected something, some pleasure, some meaningful sensation, he didn't quite know what.

So he waited, trying to nudge the right feelings alive with the details – the surprisingly familiar curve of the hedges, the stone gate-pillar and iron gatehook let into it that he had used as a target, the long bank of the rabbit-warren on which he stood and which had been the first thing he ever noticed about the hill when twenty years ago, from the distance of the village, he had said to himself 'That looks like rabbits'.

Twelve years had changed him. This land no longer recognized him, and he looked back at it coldly, as at a finally visited home-country, known only through the stories of a grandfather; felt nothing but the dullness of feeling nothing. Boredom. Then, suddenly, impatience, with a whole exasperated swarm of little anxieties about his shoes, and the spitting rain and his new suit and that sky and the two-mile trudge through the mud back to the road.

It would be quicker to go straight forward to the farm a mile away in the valley and behind which the road looped. But the thought of meeting the farmer – to be embarrassingly remembered or shouted at as a trespasser – deterred him. He saw the rain pulling up out of the distance, dragging its grey broken columns, smudging the trees and the farms.

A wave of anger went over him: anger against himself for blundering into this mud-trap and anger against the land that made him feel so outcast, so old and stiff and stupid. He wanted nothing but to get away from it as quickly as possible. But as he turned, something moved in his eye-corner. All his senses startled alert. He stopped.

Over to his right a thin, black horse was running across the ploughlands towards the hill, its head down, neck stretched out. It seemed to be running on its toes like a cat, like a dog up to no good.

From the high point on which he stood the hill dipped slightly and rose to another crested point fringed with the tops of trees, three hundred yards to his right. As he watched it, the horse ran up to that crest, showed against the sky – for a moment like a nightmarish leopard – and disappeared over the other side.

For several seconds he stared at the skyline, stunned by the unpleasantly strange impression the horse had made on him. Then the plastering beat of icy rain on his bare skull brought him to himself. The distance had vanished in a wall of grey. All around him the fields were jumping and streaming.

Holding his collar close and tucking his chin down into it he ran back over the hilltop towards the town-side, the lee-side, his feet sucking and splashing, at every stride plunging to the ankle.

This hill was shaped like a wave, a gently rounded back lifting out of the valley to a sharply crested, almost concave front hanging over the river meadows towards the town. Down this front, from the crest, hung two small woods separated by a fallow field. The near wood was nothing more than a quarry, circular, full of stones and bracken, with a few thorns and nondescript saplings, foxholes and rabbit holes. The other was rectangular, mainly a planting of scrub oak trees. Beyond the river smouldered the town like a great heap of blue cinders.

He ran along the top of the first wood and finding no shelter but the thin leafless thorns of the hedge, dipped below the crest out of the wind and jogged along through thick grass to the wood of oaks. In blinding rain he lunged through the barricades of brambles at the wood's edge. The little crippled trees were small choice in the way of shelter, but at a sudden fierce thickening of the rain he took one at random and crouched down under the leaning trunk.

Still panting from his run, drawing his knees up tightly, he watched the bleak lines of rain, grey as hail, slanting through the boughs into the clumps of bracken and bramble. He felt hidden and safe. The sound of the rain as it rushed and lulled in the wood seemed to seal him in. Soon the chilly sheet lead of his suit became a tight, warm mould, and gradually he sank into a state of comfort that was all but trance, though the rain beat steadily on his exposed shoulders and trickled down the oak trunk on to his neck.

All around him the boughs angled down, glistening, black as iron. From their tips and elbows the drops hurried steadily, and the channels of the bark pulsed and gleamed. For a time he amused himself calculating the variation in the rainfall by the variations in a dribble of water from a trembling twig-end two feet in front of his nose. He studied the twig, bringing dwarfs and continents and animals out of its scurfy bark. Beyond the boughs the blue shoal of the town was rising and falling, and darkening and fading again, in the pale, swaying backdrop of rain.

He wanted this rain to go on forever. Whenever it seemed to be drawing off he listened anxiously until it closed in again. As long as it lasted he was suspended from life and time. He didn't want to return to his sodden shoes and his possibly ruined suit and the walk back over that land of mud.

All at once he shivered. He hugged his knees to squeeze out the cold and found himself thinking of the horse. The hair on the nape of his neck prickled slightly. He remembered how it had run up to the crest and showed against the sky.

He tried to dismiss the thought. Horses wander about the countryside often enough. But the image of the horse as it had appeared against the sky stuck in his mind. It must have come over the crest just above the wood in which he was now sitting. To clear his mind, he twisted around and looked up the wood between the tree stems, to his left.

At the wood top, with the silvered grey light coming in behind it, the black horse was standing under the oaks, its head high and alert, its ears pricked, watching him.

A horse sheltering from the rain generally goes into a sort of stupor, tilts a hind hoof and hangs its head and lets its eyelids droop, and so it stays as long as the rain lasts. This horse was nothing like that. It was watching him intently, standing perfectly still, its soaked neck and flank shining in the hard light.

He turned back. His scalp went icy and he shivered. What was he to do? Ridiculous to try driving it away. And to leave the wood, with the rain still coming down full pelt, was out of the question. Meanwhile the idea of being watched became more and more unsettling until at last he had to twist around again, to see if the horse had moved. It stood exactly as before.

This was absurd. He took control of himself and turned back deliberately, determined not to give the horse one more thought. If it wanted to share the wood with him, let it. If it wanted to stare at him, let it. He was nestling firmly into these resolutions when the ground shook and he heard the crash of a heavy body coming down the wood. Like lightning his legs bounded him upright and about face. The horse was almost on top of him, its head stretching forwards, ears flattened and lips lifted back from the long yellow teeth. He got one snapshot glimpse of the red-veined eyeball as he flung himself backwards around the tree. Then he was away up the slope, whipped by oak trees as he leapt the brambles and brushwood, twisting between the close trees till he tripped and sprawled. As he fell the warning flashed through his head that he must at all costs keep his suit out of the leaf-mould, but a more urgent instinct was already rolling him violently sideways. He spun around, sat up and looked back, ready to scramble off in a flash to one side. He was panting from the sudden excitement and effort. The horse had disappeared. The wood was empty except for the drumming, slant grey rain, dancing the bracken and glittering from the branches.

He got up, furious. Knocking the dirt and leaves from his suit as well as he could he looked around for a weapon. The horse was evidently mad, had an abscess on its brain or something of the sort. Or maybe it was just spiteful. Rain sometimes puts creatures into queer states. Whatever it was, he was going to get away from the wood as quickly as possible, rain or no rain.

Since the horse seemed to have gone on down the wood, his way to the farm over the hill was clear. As he went, he broke a yard length of wrist-thick dead branch from one of the oaks, but immediately threw it aside and wiped the slime of rotten wet bark from his hands with his soaked handkerchief. Already he was thinking it incredible that the horse could have meant to attack him. Most likely it was just going down the wood for better shelter and had made a feint at him in passing – as much out of curiosity or playfulness as anything. He recalled the way horses menace each other when they are galloping around in a paddock.

The wood rose to a steep bank topped by the hawthorn hedge that ran along the whole ridge of the hill. He was pulling himself up to a thin place in the hedge by the bare stem of one of the hawthorns when he ducked and shrank down again. The swelling gradient of fields lay in front of him, smoking in the slowly crossing rain. Out in the middle of the first field, tall as a statue, and a ghostly silver in the under-cloud light, stood the horse, watching the wood.

He lowered his head slowly, slithered back down the bank and crouched. An awful feeling of helplessness came over him. He felt certain the horse had been looking straight at him. Waiting for him? Was it clairvoyant? Maybe a mad animal can be clairvoyant. At the same time he was ashamed to find himself acting so inanely, ducking and creeping about in this way just to keep out of sight of a horse. He tried to imagine how anybody in their senses would just walk off home. This cooled him a little, and he retreated farther down the wood. He would go back the way he had come, along under the hill crest, without any more nonsense.

The wood hummed and the rain was a cold weight, but he observed this rather than felt it. The water ran down inside his clothes and squelched in his shoes as he eased his way carefully over the bedded twigs and leaves. At every instant he expected to see the prick-eared black head looking down at him from the hedge above.

At the woodside he paused, close against a tree. The success of this last manoeuvre was restoring his confidence, but he didn't want to venture out into the open field without making sure that the horse was just where he had left it. The perfect move would be to withdraw quietly and leave the horse standing out there in the rain. He crept up again among the trees to the crest and peeped through the hedge.

The grey field and the whole slope were empty. He searched the distance. The horse was quite likely to have forgotten him altogether and wandered off. Then he raised himself and leaned out to see if it had come in close to the hedge. Before he was aware of anything the ground shook. He twisted around wildly to see how he had been caught. The black shape was above him, right across the light. Its whinnying snort and the spattering whack of its hooves seemed to be actually inside his head as he fell backwards down the bank, and leapt again like a madman, dodging among the oaks, imagining how the buffet would come and how he would be knocked headlong. Halfway down the wood the oaks gave way to bracken and old roots and stony rabbit diggings. He was well out into the middle of this before he realized that he was running alone.

Gasping for breath now and cursing mechanically, without a thought for his suit he sat down on the ground to rest his shaking legs, letting the rain plaster the hair down over his forehead and watching the dense flashing lines disappear abruptly into the soil all around him as if he were watching through thick plate glass. He took deep breaths in the effort to steady his heart and regain control of himself. His right trouser turn-up was ripped at the seam and his suit jacket was splashed with the yellow mud of the top field.

Obviously the horse had been farther along the hedge above the steep field, waiting for him to come out at the woodside just as he had intended. He must have peeped through the hedge – peeping the wrong way – within yards of it.

However, this last attack had cleared up one thing. He need no longer act like a fool out of mere uncertainty as to whether the horse was simply being playful or not. It was definitely after him. He picked up two stones about the size of goose eggs and set off towards the bottom of the wood, striding carelessly.

A loop of the river bordered all this farmland. If he crossed the little level meadow at the bottom of the wood, he could follow the three-mile circuit, back to the road. There were deep hollows in the river-bank, shoaled with pebbles, as he remembered, perfect places to defend himself from if the horse followed him out there.

The hawthorns that choked the bottom of the wood – some of them good-sized trees – knitted into an almost impassable barrier. He had found a place where the growth thinned slightly and had begun to lift aside the long spiny stems, pushing himself forward, when he stopped. Through the bluish veil of bare twigs he saw the familiar shape out in the field below the wood.

But it seemed not to have noticed him yet. It was looking out across the field towards the river. Quietly, he released himself from the thorns and climbed back across the clearing towards the one side of the wood he had not yet tried. If the horse would only stay down there he could follow his first and easiest plan, up the wood and over the hilltop to the farm.

Now he noticed that the sky had grown much darker. The rain was heavier every second, pressing down as if the earth had to be flooded before nightfall. The oaks ahead blurred and the ground drummed. He began to run. And as he ran he heard a deeper sound running with him. He whirled around. The horse was in the middle of the clearing. It might have been running to get out of the terrific rain except that it was coming straight for him, scattering clay and stones, with an immensely supple and powerful motion. He let out a tearing roar and threw the stone in his right hand. The result was instantaneous. Whether at the roar or the stone the horse reared as if against a wall and shied to the left. As it dropped back on its fore-feet he flung his second stone, at ten yards' range, and saw a bright mud blotch suddenly appear on the glistening black flank. The horse surged down the wood, splashing the earth like water, tossing its long tail as it plunged out of sight among the hawthorns.

He looked around for stones. The encounter had set the blood beating in his head and given him a savage energy. He could have killed the horse at that moment. That this brute should pick him and play with him in this malevolent fashion was more than he could bear. Whoever owned it, he thought, deserved to have its neck broken for letting the dangerous thing loose.

He came out at the woodside, in open battle now, still searching for the right stones. There were plenty here, piled and scattered where they had been ploughed out of the field. He selected two, then straightened and saw the horse twenty yards off in the middle of the steep field, watching him calmly. They looked at each other.

'Out of it!' he shouted, brandishing his arm. 'Out of it! Go on!' The horse twitched its pricked ears. With all his force he threw. The stone soared and landed beyond with a soft thud. He re-armed and threw again. For several minutes he kept up his bombardment without a single hit, working himself into a despair and throwing more and more wildly, till his arm began to ache with the unaccustomed exercise. Throughout the performance the horse watched him fixedly. Finally he had to stop and ease his shoulder muscle. As if the horse had been waiting for just this, it dipped its head twice and came at him.

He snatched up two stones and roaring with all his strength flung the one in his right hand. He was astonished at the crack of the impact. It was as if he had struck a tile – and the horse actually stumbled. With another roar he jumped forward and hurled his other stone. His aim seemed to be under superior guidance. The stone struck and rebounded straight up into the air, spinning fiercely, as the horse swirled away and went careering down towards the far bottom of the field, at first with great, swinging leaps, then at a canter, leaving deep churned holes in the soil.

It turned up the far side of the field, climbing till it was level with him. He felt a little surprise of pity to see it shaking its head, and once it paused to lower its head and paw over its ear with its fore-hoof as a cat does.

'You stay there!' he shouted. 'Keep your distance and you'll not get hurt.'

And indeed the horse did stop at that moment, almost obediently. It watched him as he climbed to the crest.

The rain swept into his face and he realized that he was freezing, as if his very flesh were sodden. The farm seemed miles away over the dreary fields. Without another glance at the horse – he felt too exhausted to care now what it did – he loaded the crook of his left arm with stones and plunged out on to the waste of mud.

He was half-way to the first hedge before the horse appeared, silhouetted against the sky at the corner of the wood, head high and attentive, watching his laborious retreat over the three fields.

The ankle-deep clay dragged at him. Every stride was a separate, deliberate effort, forcing him up and out of the sucking earth, burdened as he was by his sogged clothes and load of stone and limbs that seemed themselves to be turning to mud. He fought to keep his breathing even, two strides in, two strides out, the air ripping his lungs. In the middle of the last field he stopped and looked around. The horse, tiny on the skyline, had not moved.

At the corner of the field he unlocked his clasped arms and dumped the stones by the gatepost, then leaned on the gate. The farm was in front of him. He became conscious of the rain again and suddenly longed to stretch out full-length under it, to take the cooling, healing drops all over his body and forget himself in the last wretchedness of the mud. Making an effort, he heaved his weight over the gate-top. He leaned again, looking up at the hill.

Rain was dissolving land and sky together like a wet water-colour as the afternoon darkened. He concentrated raising his head, searching the skyline from end to end. The horse had vanished. The hill looked lifeless and desolate, an island lifting out of the sea, awash with every tide.

Under the long shed where the tractors, plough, binders and the rest were drawn up, waiting for their seasons, he sat on a sack thrown over a petrol drum, trembling, his lungs heaving. The mingled smell of paraffin, creosote, fertilizer, dust – all was exactly as he had left it twelve years ago. The ragged swallows' nests were still there tucked in the angles of the rafters. He remembered three dead foxes hanging in a row from one of the beams, their teeth bloody.

The ordeal with the horse had already sunk from reality. It hung under the surface of his mind, an obscure confusion of fright and shame, as after a narrowly-escaped street accident. There was a solid pain in his chest, like a spike of bone stabbing, that made him wonder if he had strained his heart on that last stupid burdened run. Piece by piece he began to take off his clothes, wringing the grey water out of them, but soon he stopped that and just sat staring at the ground, as if some important part had been cut out of his brain.

PENELOPE MORTIMER

PENELOPE MORTIMER (née Fletcher) Probably best known for her novel The Pumpkin Eater *(1962), which was made into a successful film. Penelope Mortimer has relentlessly recorded the tensions, the failures in communication, the anger and betrayals in marriage. She has been film critic for* The Observer.

I Told You So

The parents went down the cliff by the path. It was a high cliff, and the path was steep. The concrete slabs that made it were broken and rough. Laura's hands were deep in her coat pockets; her chin was jammed into her collar. She took the great, lolloping strides that were made essential by the steepness of the path and the fact that she was wearing rubber boots. She wheeled the corners of her heel, savagely, with an impression of speed.

Geoffrey followed more cautiously. He was wearing a dark grey suit, because at three o'clock he was catching the train back to London. It was Laura who had insisted that they came to the beach, in order to fill in the hour that remained before it was time to leave for the station. He could have occupied himself perfectly well by reading the Sunday newspapers and checking that he had remembered his razor and toothbrush. As it was, he was certain he had forgotten his razor. Every Monday morning during the past four weeks, he had gone to the office unshaven or unwashed or without a collar stud. He wasn't the type to manage by himself. Laura shouldn't expect it. He worried about this as he picked his way down the path, taking small, sliding steps because of his town shoes. The whole thing made him feel ridiculous.

The three children – Sarah, Catherine, and Angie – had gone off along the cliff edge, looking for some way down more dangerous than the path. They wore red, blue, and green jackets. Their heads were swathed in warm angora scarves. They were aimed forward into the wind like figure-heads, small and sharp on the horizon on the cliff.

Below, the beach shone enormously with the clear grey light that served on this cold eastern shoulder of England for sunshine. Everything was exactly in focus. The air, without warmth or dust or colour, was strong, but did not taste of the sea. There was a fringe of dry sand just under the cliff, scattered with brittle banana skins and rusty cans, but the rest of the sand, the flat acres of it, was heavy and wet as mud. Castles made of it collapsed like snowmen, and sand puddings, if they turned out at all, were unsatisfactory. The children had long since given up digging.

They came to this part of the beach because it was far enough away from the pier to avoid the deck-chairs and bathing huts, the dusty donkeys that ambled with closed eyes backward and forward between the lifeboat and the ice-cream cart. Last week-end, on a freak afternoon without wind, Laura had allowed the children to swim. Geoffrey considered it a miracle they hadn't caught pneumonia. Geoffrey distrusted the North Sea. You could drown in a sea like that, only a few feet from the shore. It had, as he repeatedly told them, treacherous currents. They just stared at him, as though he were teaching them geography instead of trying to protect their lives.

Two or three yards above the beach, the path curved for the last time, taking a gentle gradient behind a few scrubby bushes that grew low on the face of the cliff. Hands still in her pockets, feet together, Laura jumped this small precipice, landing with her boot heels dug into the sand.

Without waiting for Geoffrey, she started off towards the sea. He, reaching the beach by the path, plodded after her.

Her jump irritated and saddened him. He knew that it was a gesture – her days were full of them – but what it was meant to represent he had no idea. Why jump, risking a sprained ankle and endless inconvenience, when there was a perfectly good path? Why not hang on his arm, timidly negotiating the bend, the cracks in the concrete slabs, arriving with a little hop, if necessary, on the safer, level ground? They weren't children, to be throwing their bodies carelessly about as though they were of no value. They weren't young, for God's sake.

Laura was diminishing across the huge beach. Her footprints, unnaturally large, disappeared almost immediately in the watery sand.

'Laura!' he shouted. 'Laura!'

She dragged to a standstill, but didn't look round.

'Wait for me!' he yelled plaintively. He did not walk any faster. They were like two reels of cotton; one had unwound to its fullest extent, the other was now wrapping itself, cocoon-like, in the taut, extended thread. At last he reached her. 'Don't go rushing off like that. What d'you want to rush off like that for?'

She didn't answer, but moved her shoulders restlessly in the heavy duffel coat. Now he was here, there was no point in walking on. His presence made her realize that there was nowhere to go but the sea. He made her feel that once you had looked at the sea, walked about bravely in its shallows, thrown a pebble or two, there was nothing left to find out about it. She sighed, narrowing her eyes, peering at the distant summit of the cliff. 'Can you see the children?'

His eyes unwillingly scaled the sandy, apparently perpendicular face of the cliff, searching vaguely about on ledges, behind tufts of scrub. 'No. Do you think they're all right?'

'I should think so.'

'I don't think you should let them go off on their own like that.'

'Oh,' she said. 'Don't you?' She began playing noughts and crosses on the sand with the toe of her boot.

She didn't even listen to him any more. They might not be young, but they were at least married. He had some rights. Did she really think, because she was managing here without him, that he was unnecessary? Unnecessary to her? It was horrible. 'Look,' he said urgently, 'why don't you all come back with

me? Now. Today. There's a later train. We could catch it
easily.'

She glanced at him before drawing a line through the
noughts and crosses. 'Don't be silly.'

'But you've been here a month, for God's sake. You don't
know what hell it is in London.'

'Of course it isn't.' She spoke briskly, in the same way she
told the children how tremendously they enjoyed school. Then,
looking up, she said with pleasure, 'Oh, there they are.'

The red and green jackets were small, bold squares of
colour against the sky. The wind pulled at the ends of the
angora scarves.

'They're not going to try and get down *there* are they?' he
asked uneasily.

'It looks like it.'

'But they can't! It's far too steep.'

'Of course they can. It isn't steep at all.'

'It looks dangerous.'

'Oh, my God!' She turned away from him, her hands
clenched in her pockets.

'Well, don't be stupid. Do you want them to kill themselves?'

'Do you *think*,' she demanded, swerving round with arms
spread wide in despair, 'that I want them to kill themselves?'

'You don't exactly go out of your way to prevent it.'

Their movements on the vast, empty beach were clumsy and
pointless; they blundered about as though they were blind.
Laura rushed away from him, and then, without having
reached any destination, stopped. Supposing it is dangerous,
she thought. But it can't be. But, supposing, for once, he is
right? She cupped her hands round her mouth. 'Can you get
down?' she shouted cheerfully.

The two children waved, their legs dangling over the edge.

'Where's Angie?'

They pointed back along the cliff.

'Wait for her!' Geoffrey howled. 'Wait for Angie!'

The children seemed to shrug their shoulders, then slithered off the edge of the cliff and began plunging and sliding down towards the beach. They were quite safe. To them, their parents looked like two minutely circling beetles, their small fury inaudible.

'They heard me,' Geoffrey said. 'They distinctly heard me tell them to wait for Angie.'

'No. They didn't.'

'They heard me, and they blatantly disobeyed. I congratulate you, Laura. You're doing a wonderful job. Really wonderful.'

'Oh, Geoffrey . . .' She felt trapped with him on the huge beach. Could it really be possible that even here, with the great light sky and the sea that stretched, she vaguely believed, to Russia, he could make her feel as though they were in a small city room – doorless, windowless, the only air the warm, wasted breath of their quarrelling? She turned as though to ask him this.

He mistook her look of despair for love, for contrition at making him so unhappy. He grabbed at her arm. 'Laura,' he said. 'Look, Laura.'

'Yes?'

'Look, I've to go in a little while. Couldn't we . . .'

'Couldn't we what?'

Her face was frozen again. She froze at the touch of his hand, but he didn't realize this. She hates me, he thought. She really hates me. But why? Why? What have I done wrong? The wind blew a heavy strand of hair across her eyes. He released her from it, gently replacing the hair, tucking it behind her ear. For the first time, he dimly realized that if she hated him, she suffered, and that what she felt was, now, perhaps unalterable. 'Come back with me,' he said.

'Why?'

'I need you.'

'What for?'

It was impossible to subdue his impatience. 'What do you mean, "What for?"? Of course I need you. I can't stand living alone. You know I can't.'

'Oh,' she said. 'I see.'

She looked back towards the cliff. He realized that she was suddenly dispirited. As she dwindled inside herself into someone old and resigned and tired of fighting, he felt, unaware of the reason, a drabness in the afternoon. It was, of course, Sunday. The train would be slow. And yet when he got there, the telephone would be waiting, yesterday's letters, the bottle of Scotch he had bought last Wednesday evening. He would have the bathroom to himself and could go to sleep without apologizing. It wouldn't be too bad after all.

Apologizing? Good God, what had he got to apologize for?

'There's Angie,' Laura said.

The two elder children were half-way down the cliff. Angie had appeared at the top and was looking down. She succeeded, so small and motionless in her blue jacket, in storming the emptiness that her parents had failed to disturb. Her reluctance, her uncertainty and fear were so powerful that she became, without making a sound, the centre of the vast landscape. Her sisters, clinging like spiders to the soft cliff wall, craned their necks. The parents stood with their faces raised, stricken with doubt.

'She'll never make it,' Geoffrey said. 'Tell her to go back and come down the path.'

Laura said nothing.

'Will you tell her?' Geoffrey demanded. 'Will you please tell her before she breaks her neck?'

'She'll be all right,' Laura said quietly.

'All right? Are you crazy? Can't you see she's frightened?' He began waving both arms. 'Go back!' he shouted. 'Come down by the path!'

The child did not move. Sarah and Catherine, curious at all

the fuss, peered down over their shoulders. Sarah lost her grip and slithered a few feet in a flurry of sand.

'There you are!' Geoffrey screamed. 'There you are! They'll kill themselves!' He started off towards the cliff, slowly and urgently, like a man in a dream.

He mustn't do it, Laura thought. He mustn't. She meant that he mustn't make them mean and timid, that he must allow his children to be brave and not imprison them in the small room, the cosy cell in which they, the parents, inched through their narrow lives. All this was not considered but sprung violently out of her as she watched the paunchy city man struggling across the sand, the wind flattening the neat creases of his trousers.

'Don't!' she shouted. 'Geoffrey! Don't!' She began to run.

As she caught up with him, he shouted, 'You're crazy!' foolishly wasting his breath, pounding on.

'Leave her alone, Geoffrey! Please!'

'Why?'

'Let her try,' she implored. 'At least let her try!'

He stopped, making a megaphone of his hands. 'Go back!' he yelled. 'You can't do it, Angie! Go back!'

The child sat down on the brink of the cliff.

Laura stood still. She stared up at the child. Go on, she urged her soundlessly. Go on, Angie. You can do it.

'Stop her!' Geoffrey was shouting, signalling wildly to Sarah and Catherine high above him. 'Stop her!'

Go on, Laura insisted with tenderness. Please, Angie. Jump.

With sudden decision, the child jumped, tumbling and scrabbling down the sandy wall until she found a foothold. Then, rather shakily, she stood and began to pick her way down. Geoffrey, who had reached the bottom of the cliff, made a few ineffectual attempts to pull himself up by the insecure scrub. Laura could hear him railing furiously against Sarah and Catherine. Lolling above him on a hump of grass, they seemed to look at him sympathetically but without much interest. Accepting at last that Angie was far enough down to be safe, he gave up. He stood beating the sand off his suit, shaking it out of the cuffs of his trousers. Then, with furious dignity, he walked over to Laura.

She was smiling, hugging her coat round her hips. 'Well,' she said. 'She did it. I told you so.'

'All right,' he said testily. 'Angie climbed down a cliff. What does that prove?'

'Prove?' Do you really mean, her look asked, that you don't know?

'Yes,' he insisted savagely. 'Yes. What does it prove? That you encourage your children to break their necks, that's what it proves. For nothing. Teaching them to be bloody melo-dramatic show-offs like yourself.'

'Oh,' she said. She looked vaguely away. The wind whipped her hair across her face again, and she pushed it back, as though this, and nothing else, troubled her. 'Is that what you think?'

'Why *can't* you be reasonable?' he demanded.

'I'm sorry,' she said lightly. She was watching Angie, cer-tain now, running down the cliff as though it were a staircase.

'Why don't you come back to London, so that we can live an ordinary, sensible life?'

'Because we've taken a house here,' she said absently. 'Because it's the holidays and the summer, and the children like it. Because . . .'

'All right,' he snapped. 'All right. I know all that, for God's sake.'

'Well, then,' she said softly, as though dismissing him, as though this were all.

They began walking slowly back towards the path. Sarah and Catherine were climbing down from their perch. In a few moments they would be on the beach, and whatever anguish, whatever frustration had been hinted at would again be left unresolved. A tremendous reluctance dragged at Geoffrey's feet, weighed down his shoulders. 'It's this blasted place,' he said. 'It wasn't like this before.'

'Before when?'

'The other summers you've been away.'

'It was always like this before. We were younger, that's all.'

He stopped, stamping his foot in fury. It was like slamming a swing door; the wet sand made no sound, even his footprint immediately disappeared.

'Why, *why* will you dramatize everything? Of course we weren't younger. What the hell do you mean?'

'Last year,' she said, 'I should have thought we were younger. Angie was only six. I remember. You wouldn't let her ride on a donkey, in case she fell off.' She looked up at him sidewise, coldly, without smiling.

'A year doesn't make all that difference. You're sending me back to London without one sign of affection, do you realize that? Without one civil word? Simply because I'd sooner have my children alive than dead. Simply because I want a sensible, ordinary life instead of all this ...' He swept around at the sea, the placid beach, the soft, harmless cliffs; he took in the children, balancing on the edge of the last eight-foot drop, and returned the angry, boomerang glance to his wife. She met his stare calmly, knowing what he saw.

'This what?' she asked. Her pale lips were dried by the sea air; her body, inside the heavy, almost armoured clothes, was cramped with disuse. She lived in her clothes in restricted, solitary confinement. 'Well?' She repeated patiently, 'This what?'

'Hooliganism,' he said, as though the curious word had been made for him at that moment. 'Ridiculous hooliganism.'

A thin cheer came from the cliff. They turned and saw Angie edging herself down the last few feet. Sarah and Catherine were already on the beach. They stood with straddled legs, the seats of their jeans baboon-orange from the sand.

'Jolly good!' they shouted, in their precise, cultured voices. 'Jolly good, Angie!'

'Well,' Geoffrey mumbled. 'I must go. I don't suppose I need bother to say good-bye. They won't notice the difference. Good-bye, Laura.'

'Of course you must say goodbye.' She took his arm, as though he were a shy guest at a cocktail party. When he's gone, she thought, I can climb the cliff too. 'Of course you must say good-bye,' she repeated, suddenly gushing.

'Well.' He raised his voice in a dismal shout. 'Good-bye, everyone! See you on Friday!'

Sarah and Catherine turned and waved. Angie turned and waved. There was a small explosion of sand, the flash of a blue jacket, then – while the smiles still hung on their faces – scream after scream, the child writhing and arching herself at the bottom of the cliff, a few clods of sand falling after her in a dwarf landslide.

They both ran towards her. A tuft of grass she had been clinging to had given way; she was still holding a fistful of it. She had fallen perhaps four feet, hardly more than her own height.

'She fell,' Sarah said anxiously. 'Just that little way. She fell.'

'Of course she fell!' Geoffrey wailed. 'Of course she did!' He knelt down and tried to take the child in his arms. She screamed terribly, twisting away from him.

'It's her leg,' Catherine said excitedly. 'Look it's her leg!'

The child's jeans had wrinkled up to her knees. Laura, kneeling beside Geoffrey, saw the shin-bone sticking up like a piece of snapped celery under the taut, sandy skin.

'I think it's broken,' she said dully. 'Geoffrey. I think it's broken.'

For a moment he turned and looked at her. His face was

grey with distress, but his eyes – the tired, disappointed eyes – were shining. They were lit with triumph. He's glad, she thought incredulously. He doesn't know it, but he is actually glad.

'I told you she'd fall,' he said quietly. 'I told you so.'

He gathered up the child and, without waiting for Laura, Sarah, or Catherine, began climbing very slowly, very carefully up the cliff path. His shoes slipped from time to time on the concrete. He tested every step before relying on it. He did not attempt to comfort the child. He allowed her to cry, carrying her with great pride and caution, as though she were a treasure he had won, a rare and valuable hostage.

BILL NAUGHTON

BILL NAUGHTON (1910–) Born in County Mayo, Ireland, but soon after his birth his parents moved to Bolton in Lancashire. Left school at fourteen, became mill-worker, coal-heaver. Out of work during the Depression of the 1930s, he educated himself in public libraries. He began writing short stories for magazines during the Second World War. Success allowed him to give up working as a lorry-driver to write full-time. Late Night on Watling Street, *the collection from which 'Weaver's Knot' comes, was published in 1959. The story uses Naughton's memory of his first embarrassed job as a fourteen-year-old working in a weaving shed 'among all the women'.*

Another very popular collection of his stories, The Goalkeeper's Revenge *(1961) and several highly successful plays,* Spring and Port Wine, Alfie *(which reappeared as both a film and novel) and* All in Good Time *(filmed as* The Family Way*) have established his reputation.*

Weaver's Knot

A deafening din of machinery halted young Harry Ackers on the threshold of the weaving shed. It hit him the moment he pushed open the old thick door, and so he stood there, choked right up to the gullet it seemed, with fear and foreboding, until the door, weighted by an old cast-iron cogwheel, gave him a brusque sideways shove, as much as to say 'Either come in or get out.' He went in.

Hundreds of looms palpitated with one solid thunderous racket beneath the vast low ceilinged shed, and under the coarse glare of gaslight stood the weavers – long lines of them, all women, both old and young, stopping and starting looms, changing shuttles with a flick of the hand, and turning from one machine to another to give anxious and stopping caresses to the tight newborn cloth that emerged from warp and weft.

'*Who do you want, luv?*'

'Eh?' Harry gave a startled turn. A small freckled-face woman had seemed to fire the words softly into his ear. 'Eh? Oh, sorry, I want—' he began to shout, but his voice made no impression against the volume of noise, and he stopped.

'Who?' she asked, putting a hand on his shoulder. The one word tickled his ear.

'Mester Hambull,' he said, 'th' overlooker.'

She was watching his lips, and now she pointed a finger to a man on a workbench in the corner. 'That's Eddie,' she said.

'Ta,' said Harry, 'ta very much.'

He went across to the squat figure perched fast asleep on the bench. Two hunched-up shoulders, a big head sunk on a chest that showed hairy and thick at the open shirt, two fat folded arms and a stubby hand clutching a steel spanner, and down the front of the bench dangled short legs in oily blue overalls. Below the neb of the greasy cap were two delicately closed eyes, bushy brows, a large shapely nose and a full grey moustache. Harry watched the lift and fall of the chest, and looked with silent wonder at the sleeping face, oblivious of all the din. Preparing himself for what he should say when the man woke up, Harry quietly cleared his throat. Instantly at the sound the man woke up. He jumped off the bench with a roar:

'Urroww . . . !' he growled, blinking up at the tall lad. 'Wut game, eh? eh? wut game art up to? eh? wut's the big idea? who are tha, anyway? eh? who?'

'H-harry Ackers.'

'Eh? who? wut caper art up to i' my shed, eh?'

'Manager sent me.'

'Eh? wut art slummockin' round my bench for?' asked the man.

'I told you that Charlie Burgess, t'manager, sent me,' retorted Harry. 'He sent me to you for you to find a weaver for me, to learn me weaving afore I can go an' work as an apprentice in t'mechanic's shop.'

'Wut the 'ell does Chey Burgess think he's on?' the man asked. 'Anyway, that means "teach". Learning is wut tha does thyself, if tha has sense enough.'

I could have told you that, thought Harry, only I didn't want to show off. I was talking at thy level.

'Right,' went on the man, 'tha'd better follow me.'

The stocky figure strode down the narrow alleyway, brushing casually past thick whirring leather straps, and ignoring the vicious swinging picking sticks. Harry followed rashly behind, until a knock on the elbow gave rise to a timid caution. The man turned suddenly into a side alleyway. He went up to a woman weaver and touched her gently on the shoulder. Harry caught a glimpse of her – it was the freckle-faced woman. The man said something to her and then pointed to Harry. She nodded her head and smiled at the boy.

'I'm puttin' thee wi' Hetty Dale here,' shouted the man. 'See tha does wut she tells thee – or else tha'll have me to contend with.'

He was making off when he turned unexpectedly and came back, came close up to the boy, and spoke intimately to him:

'How old are you?'

'Fifteen an' a bit.'

'Thy first job?' he asked, glancing at the rosy cheeks.

'Aye,' said Harry.

The man gave a keen look into his eyes: 'Me an' thee, lad,' he remarked, 'we'll be the only two men in the entire shed. A shedful of women, see.' He gave a warning tap of a spanner to Harry on the shoulder: 'I'm t'gaffer here,' he added, 'an' let me give thee a tip – no wenching! I won't stand for it.'

For a moment Harry was dazed. He hadn't quite understood the words, but instinctively he had sensed the feeling behind them. He felt a strange ugly gush of emotion come up into his mouth. 'Eh, hello, luv,' the freckled woman greeted him. 'Ee, you look a bit sick you do. Here, have a sup of water – if you don't mind drinking out of my mug.' Trembling he took the mug from her hands and gulped the water. He was thirsty suddenly, but couldn't swallow properly. He felt exhausted from the hatred, adult and blind, that had sprung up in him. It even made him dizzy in the head. '*Me an' thee – men – women – I'm t'gaffer – no wenching.*' Hetty helped him off with his jacket and he began to roll up the sleeves of the working shirt his mother had bought him the day before.

It seemed to him that Hetty moved like a sprite. She darted about the alleyway from one loom to another, and slowfootedly he followed. Often he would lose sight of the head of pale yellow hair blobbed with cotton, when suddenly from between the reeds the two green eyes, gay and bright, would startle him. After her wash before going home she looked very pretty, with her smooth gleaming hair and delicate skin. And sometimes she changed her blouse, and came to work in her best coat, and then Harry could hardly keep his eyes off her.

'Going to meet your boy?' he asked her one day.

'Pooh – if you haven't got a boy at thirty-one,' she said, 'you never will have.'

'Are you thirty-one?'

'I am, luv,' she said, 'an' never been kicked, kissed or run over.'

'Ee, I wouldn't ha' thought it,' said Harry. 'I mean that you were that age – I allus thought thirty was old.'

It was the atmosphere of intimacy between them that made the job bearable for Harry. All day long they occupied the same narrow alley, two feet wide and ten feet long; their heads bent together over the same cloth, their bodies brushed by each other every minute or two, their hands touched, and they 'kissed' the same shuttle. Often Harry would press his mouth to the tiny hole in the shuttle and suck and suck without the cotton coming through, then Hetty would playfully snatch it from him and at the touch of her lips the thread would spring out of the hole.

'It's your mouth, Hetty,' he said one day, 'that magnetizes even t'cotton.'

One thing that eluded Harry was the 'weaver's knot'. It was a knot tied in a special way, to repair a broken end in the warp, and Harry's thick fingers couldn't master it. Hetty would go behind the warp as he struggled, lean over him and bring an arm over each shoulder, and her sure hands would take his fumbling ones and make them tie a knot. But when Harry felt her soft cheek against his, it seemed that the sight slipped from his eyes, and he couldn't make out what the cotton ends were doing. Then one day it chanced that just as Hetty was bringing her arms over his shoulders his fingers should happen to tie the knot. 'Ee, luv,' she laughed into his ear, 'you tied your first weaver's knot. You deserve a reward—' and she turned

Harry's face towards her and gave him a kiss on the mouth. A moment later, as she bent to draw the end through the reed, and saw the boy's tense face, she shook her head: 'Hetty, you didn't ought ha' done it,' she told herself.

Harry had felt aware always of Eddie Hambull's presence in the shed, and after the kiss he became more sensitive to it. Often he would get a glimpse of him at his bench, and he would get a feeling of being in a jungle, he a young growing lion and Hambull an old overgrown lion, and all the weavers lionesses. When the man passed the end of the alley the hair or something stiffened at the back of Harry's neck.

Most afternoons, and especially Fridays, Hetty would start the singing off in the shed. Her voice fascinated Harry, for she could pitch it so that it rose with a ghostly sweetness above the din of the machinery, and soon all the shed would join in – mostly in hymns such as 'Abide With Me'. Harry realized that there was no one in the world he thought of as he did of Hetty.

Hambull moved Harry to two looms of his own, but since these were next to Hetty's four looms he didn't mind. She still gave him a lift, helped to keep the looms going, and charged against him when he got in her way. And Harry liked to buy a bar of fruit-and-nut chocolate and give it to her when they brought the morning cocoa round.

'No thanks, luv,' she shook her head one morning, 'I don't feel like eating anything.'

'Are you all right?' asked Harry anxiously. 'You haven't been looking yourself lately, Hetty. An' I never hear you singing now. Have you just come over funny?'

Hetty looked up and smiled at him: 'Bend down,' she said. He did, and she whispered in his ear: 'I'm going to have a baby.'

Harry stared at her, unspeaking.

She asked: 'Know who's the father?'

He shook his head.

She pointed a finger at him:

'You!'

'Me!'

'Yes, you—' pouted Hetty. 'It must have happened that day you kissed me behind the looms. I've never felt the same since.' Seeing his worried expression she touched her heart: 'Cross me heart, Harry Ackers, I won't tell a soul. But let it be a lesson to you.'

Harry went back to his work in wonderment. He knew perfectly well that a woman didn't have a baby when you kissed her behind a loom – but there was something different about this case. These last months Hetty had spent more time with him than with anybody, and she had never been out of his thoughts, and he had kissed her, or she had kissed him – and all that couldn't mean nothing. In some virgin way Harry felt himself the father of the child Hetty carried.

From then on the job of weaving became easy. He forgot all dissatisfaction and tackled things with a new spirit. He ran for Hetty's cocoa, brought her baskets of cops, and often gave a matey glance over her looms, and handled his own with ease. Until one day he put two shuttles in one of his looms, and after the smash had to go and bring Hambull. 'Don't worry,' Hetty told him, 'because you never make a weaver until you put two shuttles in.' But Eddie Hambull thought different.

'Bladderhead!' he roared at Harry, 'd'you think I've no more to do than wet-nurse thee?'

Harry could have grabbed the man at his hairy throat, but instead he thought of Hetty and tended his other loom. The repairs did not take long, and when Harry came back early at dinner time Hetty was piecing up the last few ends in the quiet deserted shed.

'Give me a lift with the weights,' she called to him, 'an' keep your eye out for the factory inspector – or else we'll get sacked for working in the dinner time.'

They hurried behind the loom and bent to lift the heavy weights which kept the warp at a certain tension. Suddenly Harry heard a groan.

'Oh, what's up, Hetty?' he cried.

'I've hurt me, luv,' she whispered. 'Help me round to my box.'

'Shall I fetch woman from t'welfare room?' he asked.

'No,' said Hetty, 'go an' tell Eddie.'

'Who – Hambull?'

'Yes. He's gaffer.'

Harry ran off for the overlooker, and found him putting on his blue slop. 'Hetty Dale's hurt herself,' he blurted out.

'Hetty? – hurt herself?'

'Aye, she were givin' me a lift with the weights,' said Harry.

'Get out me way,' roared the man, thrusting past Harry and running down the alley.

'Wut's up? Wut have you done?' he shouted at Hetty. 'Liften flamin' weights – have you no more sense?' He turned to Harry: 'Hy thee – dash off to Joe Key an' tell him have the firm's car ready. Say one of my weavers has been taken bad.' And with that he put his powerful arm round Hetty and almost lifted her along the alley.

Harry went to work the next day only because he was drawn to the job and the alley, because of their comforting associations of Hetty. Often his eyes turned to her four looms, standing in queer idleness, and he imagined her there.

Two weavers were having a lip conversation across the shed, and Harry detecting the word 'Hetty' watched their lips, for he was quick at following the words.

'Last night at ten o'clock in hospital.'

'So I heard. Stillborn.'

'But she's all right.'

Harry felt a pain tighten at his heart. He was turning his eyes from the conversation when he caught the word 'Hambull'.

'It were a lucky let off for him!'

'Fancy! And it would have been his first.'

'At fifty-five!'

'Wife's an invalid.'

'Men always come best off.'

'Woman has to pay.'

Harry saw a drop of cold sweat fall from his forehead on the warp. Hambull! Ugly old Hambull. How could Hetty have? He straightened up, went round the alley and put on his jacket, knocked off the looms, and went off. At the end of the alley he came face to face with the man.

'Where are you off to?' he asked.

'I'm leaving,' said Harry.

'Wut?'

'I'm chuckin' it. I've had enough.'

Harry saw a sudden change come over the man's face as he put his hand on his shoulder and took him over to his bench.

'I suppose it's over my shouting at thee yes'day,' he said. 'Lad, tha'll punish thyself all through life.'

'How come?'

'Tha takes things to heart. I'm t'same myself.' He brought his face close to Harry's: 'I've just had a thing happen me that I can't tell thee or nob'dy else about, but I will say this – I've suffered the loss of a life's hope. I were young yest'day – now I'm an old man.'

Harry saw the man's face shed its ugliness as the deep emotion filled his blue eyes. He realized that his own sense of loss was only a sickly moment beside the desolation on the face before him.

'And where art going, lad?'

'Navy. I've turned fifteen and a half.'

'Then tha'll be going to sea.'

'Aye, to sea.'

'There's nowt here for me,' spoke the man. 'I wish – I wish I were coming wi' thee.'

'Aye,' Harry was surprised to hear himself say as he shook the thick hand, 'I wish you were, Eddie.'

ROALD DAHL

ROALD DAHL (1916–   ) Born in South Wales of Norwegian parents. Educated at Repton School and at eighteen went to work for Shell in Africa. Served as an RAF fighter-pilot in the Second World War. He has written several delightfully fantastic children's books; Charlie and the Chocolate Factory *(1964), the best known, has also been a successful film.*

Apart from these he has only published short stories: Over to You *(1946),* Someone Like You *(1953),* Kiss Kiss *(1959). His work is characterized by a 'black humour', and he is a master of shock and suspense, seeming to penetrate the psychology of the reader as acutely as he does that of his own characters. His stories have enjoyed worldwide acclaim.*

He is married to Patricia Neal, the film actress, and they and their children now live in England.

The Great Automatic Grammatizator

'Well, Knipe, my boy. Now that it's all finished, I just called you in to tell you I think you've done a fine job.'

Adolph Knipe stood still in front of Mr Bohlen's desk. There seemed to be no enthusiasm in him at all.

'Aren't you pleased?'

'Oh yes, Mr Bohlen.'

'Did you see what the papers said this morning.'

'No sir, I didn't.'

The man behind the desk pulled a folded newspaper towards him, and began to read: 'The building of the great automatic computing engine, ordered by the government some time ago, is now complete. It is probably the fastest electronic calculating machine in the world today. Its function is to satisfy the ever-increasing need of science, industry, and administration for rapid mathematical calculations which, in the past, by traditional methods, would have been physically impossible, or would have required more time than the problems justified. The speed with which the new engine works, said Mr John Bohlen, head of the firm of electrical engineers mainly responsible for its construction, may be grasped by the fact that it can provide the correct answer in five seconds to a problem that would occupy a mathematician for a month. In three minutes, it can produce a calculation that by hand (if it were possible) would fill half a million sheets of foolscap paper. The automatic computing engine uses pulses of electricity, generated at the rate of a million a second, to solve all calculations that resolve themselves into addition, subtraction, multiplication, and division. For practical purposes there is no limit to what it can do ...'

Mr Bohlen glanced up at the long, melancholy face of the younger man. 'Aren't you proud, Knipe? Aren't you pleased?'

'Of course, Mr Bohlen.'

'I don't think I have to remind you that your own contribution, especially to the original plans, was an important one. In fact, I might go so far as to say that without you and some of your ideas, this project might still be on the drawing-boards today.'

Adolph Knipe moved his feet on the carpet, and he watched the two small white hands of his chief, the nervous fingers playing with a paper-clip, unbending it, straightening out the hairpin curves. He didn't like the man's hands. He didn't like his face either, with the tiny mouth and the narrow purple-coloured lips. It was unpleasant the way only the lower lip moved when he talked.

'Is anything bothering you, Knipe? Anything on your mind?'

'Oh no, Mr Bohlen. No.'

'How would you like to take a week's holiday? Do you good. You've earned it.'

'Oh, I don't know, sir.'

The older man waited, watching this tall, thin person who stood so sloppily before him. He was a difficult boy. Why couldn't he stand up straight? Always drooping and untidy, with spots on his jacket, and hair falling all over his face.

'I'd like you to take a holiday, Knipe. You need it.'

'All right, sir. If you wish.'

'Take a week. Two weeks if you like. Go somewhere warm. Get some sunshine. Swim. Relax. Sleep. Then come back, and we'll have another talk about the future.'

Adolph Knipe went home by bus to his two-room apartment He threw his coat on the sofa, poured himself a drink of whisky, and sat down in front of the typewriter that was on the table. Mr Bohlen was right. Of course he was right. Except that he didn't know the half of it. He probably thought it was a woman. Whenever a young man gets depressed, everybody thinks it's a woman.

He leaned forward and began to read through the half-finished sheet of typing still in the machine. It was headed 'A Narrow Escape', and it began *'The night was dark and stormy, the wind whistled in the trees, the rain poured down like cats and dogs . . .'*

Adolph Knipe took a sip of whisky, tasting the malty-bitter flavour, feeling the trickle of cold liquid as it travelled down his throat and settled in the top of his stomach, cool at first, then spreading and becoming warm, making a little area of warmness in the gut. To hell with Mr John Bohlen anyway. And to hell with the great electrical computing machine. To hell with . . .

At exactly that moment, his eyes and mouth began slowly to open, in a sort of wonder, and slowly he raised his head and became still, absolutely motionless, gazing at the wall opposite with his look that was more perhaps of astonishment than of wonder, but quite fixed now, unmoving and remaining thus for forty, fifty, sixty seconds. Then, gradually (the head still motionless), a subtle change spreading over the face, astonishment becoming pleasure, very slight at first, only around the corners of the mouth, increasing gradually, spreading out until at last the whole face was open wide and shining with extreme delight. It was the first time Adolph Knipe had smiled in many, many months.

'Of course,' he said, speaking aloud, 'it's completely ridiculous.' Again he smiled, raising his upper lip and baring his teeth in a queerly sensual manner.

'It's a delicious idea, but so impracticable it doesn't really bear thinking about at all.'

From then on, Adolph Knipe began to think about nothing else. The idea fascinated him enormously, at first because it gave him a promise – however remote – of revenging himself in a most devilish manner upon his greatest enemies. From this angle alone, he toyed idly with it for perhaps ten or fifteen minutes; then all at once he found himself examining it quite seriously as a practical possibility. He took paper and made some preliminary notes. But he didn't get far. He found himself, almost immediately, up against the old truth that a machine, however ingenious, is incapable of original thought. It can handle no problems except those that resolve themselves into mathematical terms – problems that contain one, and only one, correct answer.

This was a stumper. There didn't seem any way around it. A machine cannot have a brain. On the other hand, it *can* have a memory, can it not? Their own electronic calculator had a marvellous memory. Simply by converting electric pulses, through a column of mercury, into supersonic waves, it could store away at least a thousand numbers at a time, extracting any one of them at the precise moment it was needed. Would it not be possible, therefore, on this principle, to build a memory section of almost unlimited size?

Now what about that?

Then suddenly, he was struck by a powerful but simple little truth, and it was this: *That English grammar is governed by rules that are almost mathematical in their strictness!* Given the words, and given the sense of what is to be said, then there is only one correct order in which those words can be arranged.

No, he thought, that isn't quite accurate. In many sentences there are several alternative positions for words and phrases, all of which may be grammatically correct. But what the hell. The theory itself is basically true. Therefore, it stands to reason that an engine built along the lines of the electrical computer could be adjusted to arrange words (instead of numbers) in their right order according to the rules of grammar. Give it the verbs, the nouns, the adjectives, the pronouns, store them in the memory section as a vocabulary, and arrange for them to be extracted as required. Then feed it with plots and leave it to write the sentences.

There was no stopping Knipe now. He went to work immediately, and there followed during the next few days a period of intense labour. The living-room became littered with sheets of paper: formulae and calculations; lists of words, thousands and thousands of words; the plots of stories, curiously broken up and subdivided; huge extracts from *Roget's Thesaurus*; pages filled with the first names of men and women; hundreds of surnames taken from the telephone directory; intricate drawings of wires and circuits and switches and thermionic valves; drawings of machines that could punch holes of different shapes in little cards, and of a strange electric typewriter that could type ten thousand words a minute. Also, a kind of control panel with a series of small push-buttons, each one labelled with the name of a famous American magazine.

He was working in a mood of exultation, prowling around the room amidst this littering of paper, rubbing his hands together, talking out loud to himself; and sometimes, with a sly curl of the nose, he would mutter a series of murderous imprecations in which the word 'editor' seemed always to be present. On the fifteenth day of continuous work, he collected the papers into two large folders which he carried – almost at a run – to the offices of John Bohlen Inc., electrical engineers.

Mr Bohlen was pleased to see him back.

'Well Knipe, good gracious me, you look a hundred per cent better. You have a good holiday? Where'd you go?'

He's just as ugly and untidy as ever, Mr Bohlen thought. Why doesn't he stand up straight? He looks like a bent stick. 'You look a hundred per cent better, my boy.' I wonder what he's grinning about. Every time I see him, his ears seem to have got larger.

Adolph Knipe placed the folders on the desk. 'Look, Mr Bohlen!' he cried. 'Look at these!'

Then he poured out his story. He opened the folders and pushed the plans in front of the astonished little man. He talked for over an hour, explaining everything, and when he had finished, he stepped back, breathless, flushed, waiting for the verdict.

'You know what I think, Knipe? I think you're nuts.' Careful now, Mr Bohlen told himself. Treat him carefully. He's valuable, this one is. If only he didn't look so awful, with that long horse face and the big teeth. The fellow had ears as big as rhubarb leaves.

'But Mr Bohlen! It'll work! I've proved to you it'll work! You can't deny that!'

'Take it easy now, Knipe. Take it easy, and listen to me.'

Adolph Knipe watched his man, disliking him more every second.

'This idea,' Mr Bohlen's lower lip was saying, 'is very ingenious – I might almost say brilliant – and it only goes to confirm my opinion of your abilities, Knipe. But don't take it too seriously. After all, my boy, what possible use can it be to us? Who on earth wants a machine for writing stories? And where's the money in it, anyway? Just tell me that.'

'May I sit down, sir?'

'Sure, take a seat.'

Adolph Knipe seated himself on the edge of a chair. The older man watched him with alert brown eyes, wondering what was coming now.

'I would like to explain something, Mr Bohlen, if I may, about how I came to do all this.'

'Go right ahead, Knipe.' He would have to be humoured a little now, Mr Bohlen told himself. The boy was really valuable – a sort of genius, almost – worth his weight in gold to the firm. Just look at these papers here. Darndest thing you ever saw. Astonishing piece of work. Quite useless, of course. No commercial value. But it proved again the boy's ability.

'It's a sort of confession, I suppose, Mr Bohlen. I think it explains why I've always been so . . . so kind of worried.'

'You tell me anything you want, Knipe. I'm here to help you – you know that.'

The young man clasped his hands together tight on his lap, hugging himself with his elbows. It seemed as though suddenly he was feeling very cold.

'You see, Mr Bohlen, to tell the honest truth, I don't really care much for my work here. I know I'm good at it and all that sort of thing, but my heart's not in it. It's not what I want to do most.'

Up went Mr Bohlen's eyebrows, quick like a spring. His whole body became very still.

'You see, sir, all my life I've wanted to be a writer.'

'A writer!'

'Yes, Mr Bohlen. You may not believe it, but every bit of spare time I've had, I've spent writing stories. In the last ten years I've written hundreds, literally hundreds of short stories. Five hundred and sixty-six, to be precise. Approximately one a week.'

'Good heavens man! What on earth did you do that for?'

'All I know, sir, is I have the urge.'

'What sort of urge?'

'The creative urge, Mr Bohlen.' Every time he looked up he saw Mr Bohlen's lips. They were growing thinner and thinner, more and more purple.

'And may I ask you what you do with these stories, Knipe?'

'Well sir, that's the trouble. No one will buy them. Each time I finish one, I send it out on the rounds. It goes to one magazine after another. That's all that happens, Mr Bohlen, and they simply send them back. Its very depressing.'

Mr Bohlen relaxed. 'I can see quite well how you feel, my boy.' His voice was dripping with sympathy. 'We all go through it one time or another in our lives. But now – now that you've had proof – positive proof – from the experts themselves, from the editors, that your stories are what shall I say – rather unsuccessful, it's time to leave off. Forget it, my boy. Just forget all about it.'

'No, Mr Bohlen! No! That's not true! I *know* my stories

are good. My heavens, when you compare them with the stuff some of those magazines print – oh my word, Mr Bohlen! – the sloppy, boring stuff that you see in the magazines week after week – why, it drives me mad!'

'Now wait a minute, my boy . . .'

'Do you ever read the magazines, Mr Bohlen?'

'You'll pardon me, Knipe, but what's all this got to do with your machine?'

'Everything, Mr Bohlen, absolutely everything! What I want to tell you is, I've made a study of magazines, and it seems that each one tends to have its own particular type of story. The writers – the successful ones – know this, and they write accordingly.'

'Just a minute, my boy. Calm yourself down, will you. I don't think all this is getting us anywhere.'

'*Please*, Mr Bohlen, hear me through. It's all terribly important.' He paused to catch his breath. He was properly worked up now, throwing his hands around as he talked. The long, toothy face, with the big ears on either side, simply shone with enthusiasm, and there was an excess of saliva in his mouth which caused him to speak his words wet. 'So you see, on my machine, by having an adjustable co-ordinator between the "plot-memory" section and the "word-memory" section, I am able to produce any type of story I desire simply by pressing the required button.'

'Yes, I know, Knipe, I know. This is all very interesting, but what's the point of it?'

'Just this, Mr Bohlen. The market is limited. We've got to be able to produce the right stuff, at the right time, whenever we want it. It's a matter of business, that's all. I'm looking at it from *your* point of view now – as a commercial proposition.'

'My dear boy, it can't possibly be a commercial proposition – ever. You know as well as I do what it costs to build one of these machines.'

'Yes sir, I do. But with due respect, I don't believe you know what the magazines pay writers for stories.'

'What do they pay?'

'Anything up to twenty-five hundred dollars. It probably averages around a thousand.'

Mr Bohlen jumped.

'Yes, *sir*, it's true.'

'Absolutely impossible, Knipe! Ridiculous!'

'No sir, it's true.'

'You mean to sit there and tell me that these magazines pay out money like that to a man for . . . just for scribbling off a story! Good heavens, Knipe! Whatever next! Writers must all be millionaires!'

'That's exactly it, Mr Bohlen! That's where the machine comes in. Listen a minute, sir, while I tell you some more. I've got it all worked out. The big magazines are carrying approximately three fiction stories in each issue. Now, take the fifteen most important magazines – the ones paying the most money. A few of them are monthlies, but most of them come out every week. All right. That makes, let us say, around forty big stories being bought each week. That's forty thousand dollars. So with our machine – when we get it working properly – we can collar nearly the whole of this market!'

'My dear boy, you're mad!'

'No sir, honestly, it's true what I say. Don't you see that with volume alone we'll completely overwhelm them! This machine can produce a five-thousand word story, all typed and ready for despatch, in thirty seconds. How can the writers compete with that? I ask you, Mr Bohlen, *how*?'

At that point, Adolph Knipe noticed a slight change in the man's expression, an extra brightness in the eyes, the nostrils distending, the whole face becoming still, almost rigid. Quickly, he continued. 'Nowadays, Mr Bohlen, the hand-made article hasn't a hope. It can't possibly compete with mass-production, especially in this country – you know that.

Carpets . . . chairs . . . shoes . . . bricks . . . crockery . . . anything you like to mention – they're all made by machinery
now. The quality may be inferior, but that doesn't matter.
It's the cost of production that counts. And stories – well –
they're just another product, like carpets and chairs, and
no one cares how you produce them so long as you deliver
the goods. We'll sell them wholesale, Mr Bohlen! We'll
undercut every writer in the country! We'll corner the
market!'

Mr Bohlen edged up straighter in his chair. He was leaning
forward now, both elbows on the desk, the face alert, the small
brown eyes resting on the speaker.

'I still think it's impracticable, Knipe.'

'Forty thousand a week!' cried Adolph Knipe. 'And if we
halve the price, making it twenty thousand a week, that's still
a million a year!' And softly he added, 'You didn't get any
million a year for building the old electronic calculator, did
you, Mr Bohlen?'

'But seriously now, Knipe. D'you really think they'd buy
them?'

'Listen, Mr Bohlen. Who on earth is going to want custom-
made stories when they can get the other kind at half the
price? It stands to reason, doesn't it?'

'And how will you sell them? Who will you say has written
them?'

'We'll set up our own literary agency, and we'll distribute
them through that. And we'll invent all the names we want for
the writers.'

'I don't like it, Knipe. To me, that smacks of trickery, does
it not?'

'And another thing, Mr Bohlen. There's all manner of
valuable byproducts once you've got started. Take advertising,
for example. Beer manufacturers and people like that are willing to pay good money these days if famous writers will lend
their names to their products. Why, my heavens, Mr Bohlen!

This isn't any children's plaything we're talking about. It's big business.'

'Don't get too ambitious, my boy.'

'And another thing. There isn't any reason why we shouldn't put *your* name, Mr Bohlen, on some of the better stories, if you wished it.'

'My goodness, Knipe. What should I want that for?'

'I don't know, sir, except that some writers get to be very much respected – like Mr Erle Gardner or Kathleen Norris, for example. We've got to have names, and I was certainly thinking of using my own on one or two stories, just to help out.'

'A writer, eh?' Mr Bohlen said, musing. 'Well, it would surely surprise them over at the club when they saw my name in the magazines – the good magazines.'

'That's right, Mr Bohlen.'

For a moment, a dreamy, faraway look came into Mr Bohlen's eyes, and he smiled. Then he stirred himself and began leafing through the plans that lay before him.

'One thing I don't quite understand, Knipe. Where do the plots come from? The machine can't possibly invent plots.'

'We feed those in, sir. That's no problem at all. Everyone has plots. There's three or four hundred of them written down in that folder there on your left. Feed them straight into the "plot-memory" section of the machine.'

'Go on.'

'There are many other little refinements, too, Mr Bohlen. You'll see them all when you study the plans carefully. For example, there's a trick that nearly every writer uses, of inserting at least one long, obscure word in each story. This makes the reader think that the man is very wise and clever. So I have the machine do the same thing. There'll be a whole stack of long words stored away just for this purpose.'

'Where?'

'In the "word-memory" section,' he said, epexegetically.

Through most of that day the two men discussed the possibilities of the new engine. In the end, Mr Bohlen said he would have to think about it some more. The next morning, he was quietly enthusiastic. Within a week, he was completely sold on the idea.

'What we'll have to do, Knipe, is to say that we're merely building another mathematical calculator, but of a new type. That'll keep the secret.'

'Exactly, Mr Bohlen.'

And in six months the machine was completed. It was housed in a separate brick building at the back of the premises, and now that it was ready for action, no one was allowed near it excepting Mr Bohlen and Adolph Knipe.

It was an exciting moment when the two men – the one, short, plump, breviped – the other tall, thin, and toothy – stood in the corridor before the control panel and got ready to run off the first story. All around them were walls dividing up into many small corridors, and the walls were covered with wiring and plugs and switches and huge glass valves. They were both nervous, Mr Bohlen hopping from one foot to the other, quite unable to keep still.

'Which button?' Adolph Knipe asked, eyeing a row of small white discs that resembled the keys of a typewriter. 'You choose, Mr Bohlen. Lots of magazines to pick from – *Saturday Evening Post, Collier's, Ladies' Home Journal* – any one you like.'

'Goodness me, boy! How do I know?' He was jumping up and down like a man with hives.

'Mr Bohlen,' Adolph Knipe said gravely, 'do you realize that at this moment, with your little finger alone, you have it in your power to become the most versatile writer on this continent?'

'Listen Knipe, just get on with it, will you please – and cut out the preliminaries.'

'Okay, Mr Bohlen. Then we'll make it ... let me see – this

one. How's that?' He extended one finger and pressed down a button with the name *Today's Woman* printed across it in diminutive black type. There was a sharp click, and when he took his finger away, the button remained down, below the level of the others.

'So much for the selection,' he said. 'Now – here we go!' He reached up and pulled a switch on the panel. Immediately, the room was filled with a loud humming noise, and a crackling of electrical sparks, and the jingle of many, tiny, quickly-moving levers; and almost in the same instant, sheets of quarto paper began sliding out from a slot to the right of the control panel and dropping into a basket below. They came out quick, one sheet a second, and in less than half a minute it was all over. The sheets stopped coming.

'That's it!' Adolph Knipe cried. 'There's your story!'

They grabbed the sheets and began to read. The first one they picked up started as follows: 'Aifkjmbsaoegwcztpplnvo-qudskigt&,fuhpekanvbertyuiolkjhgfdsazxcvbnm,peruitrehdjkg-mvnb,wmsuy . . .' They looked at the others. The style was roughly similar in all of them. Mr Bohlen began to shout. The younger man tried to calm him down.

'It's all right, sir. Really it is. It only needs a little adjustment. We've got a connection wrong somewhere, that's all. You must remember, Mr Bohlen, there's over a million feet of wiring in this room. You can't expect everything to be right first time.'

'It'll never work,' Mr Bohlen said.

'Be patient, sir. Be patient.'

Adolph Knipe set out to discover the fault, and in four days' time he announced that all was ready for the next try.

'It'll never work,' Mr Bohlen said. 'I know it'll never work.'

Knipe smiled and pressed the selector button marked *Reader's Digest*. Then he pulled the switch, and again the strange, exciting, humming sound filled the room. One page of typescript flew out of the slot into the basket.

'Where's the rest?' Mr Bohlen cried. 'It's stopped! It's gone wrong!'

'No, sir, it hasn't. It's exactly rght. It's for the *Digest*, don't you see?'

This time it began: 'Fewpeopleyetknowthatarevolutionary newcurehasbeendiscoveredwhichmaywellbringpermanentrelief tosufferersofthemostdreadeddiseaseofourtime . . .' And so on.

'It's gibberish!' Mr Bohlen shouted.

'No sir, it's fine. Can't you see? It's simply that she's not breaking up the words. That's an easy adjustment. But the story's there. Look, Mr Bohlen, look! It's all there except that the words are joined together.'

And indeed it was.

On the next try a few days later, everything was perfect, even the punctuation. The first story they ran off, for a famous women's magazine, was a solid, plotty story of a boy who wanted to better himself with his rich employer. This boy arranged, so the story went, for a friend to hold up the rich man's daughter on a dark night when she was driving home. Then the boy himself, happening by, knocked the gun out of his friend's hand and rescued the girl. The girl was grateful. But the father was suspicious. He questioned the boy sharply. The boy broke down and confessed. Then the father, instead of kicking him out of the house, said that he admired the boy's resourcefulness. The girl admired his honesty – and his looks. The father promised him to be head of the Accounts Department. The girl married him.

'It's tremendous, Mr Bohlen! It's exactly right!'

'Seems a bit sloppy to me, my boy.'

'No sir, it's a seller, a real seller!'

In his excitement, Adolph Knipe promptly ran off six more stories in as many minutes. All of them – except one, which for some reason came out a trifle lewd – seemed entirely satisfactory.

Mr Bohlen was now mollified. He agreed to set up a literary

agency in an office down town, and to put Knipe in charge. In a couple of weeks, this was accomplished. Then Knipe mailed out the first dozen stories. He put his own name to four of them, Mr Bohlen's to one, and for the others he simply invented names.

Five of these stories were promptly accepted. The one with Mr Bohlen's name on it was turned down with a letter from the fiction editor saying, 'This is a skilful job, but in our opinion it doesn't quite come off. We would like to see more of this writer's work ...'Adolph Knipe took a cab out to the factory and ran off another story for the same magazine. He again put Mr Bohlen's name to it, and mailed it immediately. That one they bought.

The money started pouring in. Knipe slowly and carefully stepped up the output, and in six months' time he was delivering thirty stories a week, and selling about half.

He began to make a name for himself in literary circles as a prolific and successful writer. So did Mr Bohlen; but not quite such a good name, although he didn't know it. At the same time, Knipe was building up a dozen or more fictitious persons as promising young authors. Everything was going fine.

At this point it was decided to adapt the machine for writing novels as well as stories. Mr Bohlen, thirsting now for greater honours in the literary world, insisted that Knipe go to work at once on this prodigious task.

'I want to do a novel,' he kept saying. 'I want to do a novel.'

'And so you will, sir. And so you will. But please be patient. This is a very complicated adjustment I have to make.'

'Everyone tells me I ought to do a novel,' Mr Bohlen cried. 'All sorts of publishers are chasing after me day and night begging me to stop fooling around with stories and do something really important instead. A novel's the only thing that counts – that's what they say.'

'We're going to do novels,' Knipe told him. 'Just as many as we want. But please be patient.'

'Now listen to me, Knipe. What I'm going to do is a *serious* novel, something that'll make 'em sit up and take notice. I've been getting rather tired of the sort of stories you've been putting my name to lately. As a matter of fact, I'm none too sure you haven't been trying to make a monkey out of me.'

'A monkey, Mr Bohlen?'

'Keeping all the best ones for yourself, that's what you've been doing.'

'Oh no, Mr Bohlen! No!'

'So this time I'm going to make damn sure I write a high class intelligent book. You understand that.'

'Look, Mr Bohlen. With the sort of switchboard I'm rigging up, you'll be able to write any sort of book you want.'

And this was true, for within another couple of months, the genius of Adolph Knipe had not only adapted the machine for novel writing, but had constructed a marvellous new control system which enabled the author to pre-select literally any type of plot and any style of writing he desired. There were so many dials and levers on the thing, it looked like the instrument panel of some enormous aeroplane.

First, by depressing one of a series of master buttons, the writer made his primary decision: historical, satirical, philosophical, political, romantic, erotic, humorous, or straight. Then, from the second row (the basic buttons), he chose his theme: army life, pioneer days, civil war, world war, racial problem, wild west, country life, childhood memories, seafaring, the sea bottom, and many, many more. The third row of buttons gave a choice of literary style: classical, whimsical, racy, Hemingway, Faulkner, Joyce, feminine, etc. The fourth row was for characters, the fifth for wordage – and so on and so on – ten long rows of pre-selector buttons.

But that wasn't all. Control had also to be exercised during the actual writing process (which took about fifteen minutes per novel), and to do this the author had to sit, as it were, in the driver's seat, and pull (or push) a battery of labelled stops, as on an organ. By so doing, he was able continually to modulate or merge fifty different and variable qualities such as tension, surprise, humour, pathos, and mystery. Numerous dials and gauges on the dashboard itself told him throughout exactly how far along he was with his work.

Finally, there was the question of 'passion'. From a careful study of the books at the top of the best-seller lists for the past year, Adolph Knipe had decided that this was the most important ingredient of all – a magical catalyst that somehow or other could transform the dullest novel into a howling success – at any rate financially. But Knipe also knew that passion was powerful, heady stuff, and must be prudently dispensed – the right proportions at the right moments; and to ensure this, he had devised an independent control consisting of two sensitive sliding adjustors operated by foot-pedals, similar to the throttle and brake in a car. One pedal governed the percentage of passion to be injected, the other regulated its intensity. There was no doubt, of course – and this was the only drawback – that the writing of a novel by the Knipe method was going to be rather like flying a plane and driving a car and playing an organ all at the same time, but this did not trouble the inventor. When all was ready, he proudly escorted Mr Bohlen into the machine house and began to explain the operating procedure for the new wonder.

'Good God, Knipe! I'll never be able to do all that! Dammit, man, it'd be easier to write the thing by hand!'

'You'll soon get used to it, Mr Bohlen, I promise you. In a week or two, you'll be doing it without hardly thinking. It's just like learning to drive.'

Well, it wasn't quite as easy as that, but after many hours of practice, Mr Bohlen began to get the hang of it, and finally, late one evening, he told Knipe to make ready for running off the first novel. It was a tense moment, with the fat little man crouching nervously in the driver's seat, and the tall toothy Knipe fussing excitedly around him.

'I intend to write an important novel, Knipe.'

'I'm sure you will, sir. I'm sure you will.'

With one finger, Mr Bohlen carefully pressed the necessary pre-selector buttons:

Master button – *satirical*

Subject – *racial problem*

Style – *classical*

Characters – *six men, four women, one infant*

Length – *fifteen chapters.*

At the same time he had his eye particularly upon three organ stops marked *power, mystery, profundity.*

'Are you ready, sir?'

'Yes, yes, I'm ready.'

Knipe pulled the switch. The great engine hummed. There was a deep whirring sound from the oiled movement of fifty thousand cogs and rods and levers; then came the drumming of the rapid electrical typewriter, setting up a shrill, almost intolerable clatter. Out into the basket flew the typewritten pages – one every two seconds. But what with the noise and the excitement, and having to play upon the stops, and watch the chapter-counter and the pace-indicator and the passion-gauge, Mr Bohlen began to panic. He reacted in precisely the way a learner driver does in a car – by pressing both feet hard down on the pedals and keeping them there until the thing stopped.

'Congratulations on your first novel,' Knipe said, picking up the great bundle of typed pages from the basket.

Little pearls of sweat were oozing out all over Mr Bohlen's face. 'It sure was hard work, my boy.'

'But you got it done, sir. You got it done.'

'Let me see it, Knipe. How does it read?'

He started to go through the first chapter, passing each finished page to the younger man.

'Good heavens, Knipe! What's this!' Mr Bohlen's thin purple fish-lip was moving slightly as it mouthed the words, his cheeks were beginning slowly to inflate.

'But look here, Knipe! This is outrageous!'

'I must say it's a bit fruity, sir.'

'*Fruity*! It's perfectly revolting! I can't possibly put my name to this!'

'Quite right, sir. Quite right.'

'Knipe! Is this some nasty trick you've been playing on me?'

'Oh no, sir! No!'

'It certainly looks like it.'

'You don't think, Mr Bohlen, that you mightn't have been pressing a little hard on the passion-control pedals, do you?'

'My dear boy, how should *I* know.'

'Why don't you try another?'

So Mr Bohlen ran off a second novel, and this time it went according to plan.

Within a week, the manuscript had been read and accepted by an enthusiastic publisher. Knipe followed with one in his own name, then made a dozen more for good measure. In no time at all Adolph Knipe's Literary Agency had become famous for its large stable of promising young novelists. And once again the money started rolling in.

It was at this stage that young Knipe began to display a new talent for big business.

'See here, Mr Bohlen,' he said. 'We still got too much competition. Why don't we just absorb all the other writers in the country?'

Mr Bohlen, who now sported a bottle-green velvet jacket and allowed his hair to cover two-thirds of his ears, was quite content with things the way they were. 'Don't know what you mean, my boy. You can't just absorb writers.'

'Of course you can, sir. Exactly like Rockefeller did with his oil companies. Simply buy 'em out, and if they won't sell, squeeze 'em out. It's easy!'

'Careful now, Knipe. Be careful.'

'I've got a list here, sir, of fifty of the most successful writers in the country, and what I intend to do is offer each one of them a lifetime contract with pay. All *they* have to do is undertake never to write another word; and, of course, to let us use their names on our own stuff. How about that?'

'They'll never agree.'

'You don't know writers, Mr Bohlen. You watch and see.'

'What about the creative urge, Knipe?'

'It's bunk! All they're really interested in is the money – just like everybody else.'

In the end Mr Bohlen reluctantly agreed to give it a try, and Knipe, with his list of writers in his pocket, went off in a large chauffeur-driven Cadillac to make his calls.

He journeyed first to the man at the top of the list, a very great and wonderful writer, and he had no trouble getting into the house. He told his story and produced a suitcase full of sample novels, and a contract for the man to sign which guaranteed him so much a year for life. The man listened politely, decided he was dealing with a lunatic, gave him a drink, then firmly showed him to the door.

The second writer on the list, when he saw Knipe was serious, actually attacked him with a large metal paper-weight, and the inventor had to flee down the garden followed by such a torrent of abuse and obscenity as he had never heard before.

But it took more than this to discourage Adolph Knipe. He was disappointed but not dismayed, and off he went in his big car to seek his next client. This one was a female, famous and popular, whose fat romantic books sold by the million across the country. She received Knipe graciously, gave him tea, and listened attentively to his story.

'It all sounds very fascinating,' she said. 'But of course I find it a little hard to believe.'

'Madam,' Knipe answered. 'Come with me and see it with your own eyes. My car awaits you.'

So off they went, and in due course, the astonished lady was ushered into the machine house where the wonder was kept. Eagerly Knipe explained its workings, and after a while he even permitted her to sit in the driver's seat and practise with the buttons.

'All right,' he said suddenly, 'You want to do a book now?'

'Oh yes!' she cried. 'Please!'

She was very competent and seemed to know exactly what she wanted. She made her own pre-selections, then ran off a long, romantic, passion-filled novel. She read through the first chapter and became so enthusiastic that she signed up on the spot.

'That's one of them out of the way,' Knipe said to Mr Bohlen afterwards. 'A pretty big one too.'

'Nice work, my boy.'

'And you know *why* she signed?'

'Why?'

'It wasn't the money. She's got plenty of that.'

'Then why?'

Knipe grinned, lifting his lip and baring a long pale upper gum. 'Simply because she saw the machine-made stuff was better than her own.'

Thereafter, Knipe wisely decided to concentrate only upon mediocrity. Anything better than that – and there were so few it didn't matter much – was apparently not quite so easy to seduce.

In the end, after several months of work he had persuaded something like seventy per cent of the writers on his list to sign the contract. He found that the older ones, those who were running out of ideas and had taken to drink, were the easiest to handle. The younger people were more troublesome. They were apt to become abusive, sometimes violent when he approached them; and more than once Knipe was slightly injured on his rounds.

But on the whole, it was a satisfactory beginning. This last year – the first full year of the machine's operation – it was estimated that at least one half of all the novels and stories published in the English language were produced by Adolph Knipe upon the Great Automatic Grammatizator.

Does this surprise you?

I doubt it.

And worse is yet to come. Today, as the secret spreads, many more are hurrying to tie up with Mr Knipe. And all the time the screw turns tighter for those who hesitate to sign their names.

This very moment, as I sit here listening to the howling of my nine starving children in the other room, I can feel my own hand creeping closer and closer to that golden contract that lies over on the other side of the desk.

Give us strength, oh Lord, to let our children starve.

Acknowledgements

We are grateful to the following for permission to reproduce copyright material:

Andre Deutsch Ltd for 'The Thing without a Name' from *Miguel Street* by V. S. Naipaul; Eyre & Spottiswoode (Publishers) Ltd for 'A Summer's Reading' from *The Magic Barrel* by Bernard Malamud; Faber and Faber Ltd for 'The Rain Horse' from *Wodwo* by Ted Hughes; Farrar, Strauss & Giroux, Inc. for 'The Man Who Shot Snapping Turtles' from *Memoirs of Hecate County* by Edmund Wilson; Victor Gallancz Ltd for 'The Swimmer' from *The Brigadier and the Golf Widow* by John Cheever; The Hogarth Press Ltd for 'The Doll' by A. L. Barker from *Innocents*; Longman Paul Ltd for 'The Chaucerian' from *Collected Stories* by Frank Sargeson; Martin Secker & Warburg Ltd for 'What do Hippos Eat?' from *Such Darling Dodos* by Angus Wilson; MacGibbon & Kee Ltd for 'Weaver's Knot' from *Late Night on Watling Street* by Bill Naughton; Author's agents for 'I Told You So' from *Saturday Lunch with the Brownings* by Penelope Mortimer; Reprinted by permission of A. D. Peters & Company and 'First Confession' from *My Oedipus Complex* by Frank O'Connor; Reprinted by permission of A. D. Peters & Company; Author's agents for 'The Great Automatic Grammatizator' from *Someone Like You* by Roald Dahl published by Michael Joseph Ltd and Penguin Books Ltd © Roald Dahl 1953; George Weidenfeld & Nicolson for 'The Boss' from *Beggar My Neighbour* by Dan Jacobson; and Author's agents for 'Willy-Wagtails by Moonlight' from *The Burnt Ones* by Patrick White.

Further books in the Heritage of Literature Series

THE WESKER TRILOGY   Arnold Wesker
Edited by Andrew Best and Mark Cohen
All three plays, *Chicken Soup with Barley*, *Roots* and *I'm Talking About Jerusalem* evolve from Arnold Wesker's own life, and bear the mark of personal experience. In 1960, all three plays were performed at the Royal Court Theatre, London, and in the same year were published in a single volume.

ROOTS   Arnold Wesker
Edited by Andrew Best and Mark Cohen
Arnold Wesker concentrates a picture of an isolated rural community into a few days in the life of one family. The play had its first performance at the Belgrade Theatre in Coventry in 1959.

THE ROYAL HUNT OF THE SUN   Peter Shaffer
Edited by A. W. England
A play concerning the conquest of Peru.

SUNSET SONG   Lewis Grassic Gibbon
Edited by J. T. Low
Lewis Grassic Gibbon is one of the best known Scottish writers, and his trilogy, *A Scots Quair*, of which *Sunset Song* is the first book, is regarded as a classic of Scottish literature. *Sunset Song* captures the flavour of a rural community whose way of life was being threatened by the First World War and modern civilization.

BILLY LIAR   Keith Waterhouse
THE LONELINESS OF THE LONG-DISTANCE RUNNER   Alan Sillitoe
Edited by D. R. Elloway
Two short novels by two of the best-known post-war writers in one volume.

177

Further Books in the Heritage of Literature Series

ANIMAL FARM   George Orwell
Edited by Laurence Brander
A 'fairy story' by one of the great English political satirists.

SCIENCE FICTION   Edited by S. H. Burton
Requiem Robert Heinlein, *A Present from Joe* Eric Frank Russell, *Dark They Were and Golden-Eyed* Ray Bradbury, *Protected Species* H. B. Fyfe, *The New Wine* John Christopher, *Nightfall* Isaac Asimov, *The Windows of Heaven* John Brunner, *Youth* Isaac Asimov, *The Star* Arthur C. Clarke.

MODERN SHORT STORIES   Edited by S. H. Burton
The Secret Life of Walter Mitty and *A Couple of Hamburgers* James Thurber, *The Pedestrian* and *The Scythe* Ray Bradbury, *The Machine Stops* E. M. Forster, *Jeremy Rodock* James Schaefer, *To Build a Fire* Jack London, *The Vertical Ladder* William Sansom, *Red Letter Day* Joyce Cary, *The Real Thing* Henry James, *Miss Duveen* Walter de la Mare, *The Sugawn Chair* Sean O'Faolain.

NINE DETECTIVE STORIES   Edited by J. G. M. Merson
Mr Pemberton's Commission Freeman Wills Crofts, *The Wrong Problem* John Dickson Carr, *Tall Story* Margery Allingham, *According to the Altar Boy* Georges Simenon, *The Poisoned Dow '08* Dorothy L. Sayers, *The Thumb Mark of St Peter* Agatha Christie, *A Lesson in Crime* G. D. H. and M. Cole, *Inquest* Loel Yeo, *The Slave Detective: The Case of Cotta's Jewels* Wallace Nichols.

THIRTEEN SHORT STORIES   Edited by H. Bell
The Luncheon W. Somerset Maugham, *The Blue Bead* Norah Burke, *The Conger Eel* Liam O'Flaherty, *The Sweet Shop* E. C. Bentley, *The Voyage* Katherine Mansfield, *The Cargo of Rice* C. S. Forester, *Fear* H. E. Bates, *The Man Who Stole the Pelican* I. A. Williams, *The Loathly Opposite* John Buchan, *The Stalled Ox* 'Saki', *Quality* John Galsworthy, *The Cop and the Anthem* O. Henry, *The Diamond Maker* H. G. Wells.
With short notes and questions.

CHOSEN SHORT STORIES   Edited by G. C. Rosser
Badeni's Bank Note Frank Brownlee, *Running Wolf* Algernon Blackwood, *The Red-Headed League* Sir Arthur Conan Doyle, *The Judgement of Paris* Leonard Merrick, *The Devil and the Old Man*

Further Books in the Heritage of Literature Series

John Masefield, *The Verger* Somerset Maugham, *A Comedy of Capricorn* Morley Roberts, *The Bottle Imp* Robert Louis Stevenson.

SHORT STORIES OF THE TWENTIETH CENTURY   Edited by R. W. Jepson
The Ship that Found Herself Rudyard Kipling, *Captain Sharkey: How the Governor of Saint Kitt's Came Home* Sir Arthur Conan Doyle, *The Ghost Ship* R. B. Middleton, *The Gift of the Magi* O Henry, *The Land of the Green Ginger* Algernon Blackwood, *My Christmas Burglary* Sir A. Quiller-Couch, *Silver Circus* A. E. Coppard, *The Key* A. E. W. Mason, *A School Story* M. R. James, *The Old Lady with the Two Umbrellas* Stacy Aumonier, *The Story of Yung Chang* Ernest Bramah, *The Tremendous Adventures of Major Brown* G. K. Chesterton.

SHORT STORIES BY MODERN WRITERS   Edited by R. W. Jepson
The Rewards of Industry Richard Garnett, *An Occurrence at Owl Creek Bridge* Ambrose Bierce, *Roads of Destiny* O. Henry, *Mrs Packletide's Tiger* 'Saki', *The Fly* Katherine Mansfield, *Another Temple Gone* C. E. Montague, *The Kidnapped 'General'* Stacy Aumonier, *The Willow Plate Embellishment* Ernest Bramah, *The Invisible Man* G. K. Chesterton, *Made out of Nothing* L. P. Jacks, *The Reaping Race* Liam O'Flaherty, *Time* H. E. Bates.

TITLES IN PREPARATION

FARMER'S BOY   J. R. Allen
Edited by D. M. Budge
An autobiographical novel about a young boy growing up on a Scottish farm just before and during the First World War, this book centres on the relationship between the boy and his grandfather.

ANGLO-SAXON ATTITUDES   Angus Wilson
Edited by S. H. Burton
Angus Wilson is a prolific and well-known adult author and *Anglo-Saxon Attitudes* is acknowledged as one of the major post-war novels. The book provides social comedy in an academic setting and has a specially written introduction by the author.